Praise for Mira's Diary: Lost in Paris

"A passionate celebration of honor and integrity. Anyone interested in history, mystery, and art will be riveted by Mira's courageous journey back through time in search of justice… Fast paced and compelling."

—Newbery Medal Winner and *New York Times* bestselling author Karen Cushman

"With vividly detailed descriptions…Moss' thought-provoking tale examines the devastating effects of prejudice and intolerance…A surprise ending will leave readers anticipating Mira's next mission as she follows her mother through time and history."

—*Kirkus*

"An engrossing, diary-style blend of history, mystery, and time travel."

—*Publishers Weekly*

"A whirlwind, time-travelling tour of the city of lights—replete with firey artists, evil beauties, creepy gargoyles and vibrant sketches…all my most favorite things."

—Lisa Brown, bestselling author and illustrator of *How to Be* and *Sometimes*

"Let Moss's charming illustrations be your guide as you race headlong to a conclusion that brilliantly fuses history and mystery."

—Sue Stauffacher, author of *Donuthead*

"A delight! Part mystery, part historical fiction, part time-travel fantasy, and part art history, this page-turner introduces an important moment in the history of human rights."

—Marcia Lovelace, Librarian

Mira's Diary
HOME SWEET ROME

marissa moss

sourcebooks
jabberwocky

Sourcebooks and the colophon are registered trademarks of Sourcebooks, Inc.

Published by Sourcebooks Jabberwocky, an imprint of Sourcebooks, Inc.
P.O. Box 4410, Naperville, Illinois 60567-4410
(630) 961-3900
Fax: (630) 961-2168
www.jabberwockykids.com

Library of Congress Cataloging-in-Publication data is on file with the publisher.

Source of Production: Bang Printing, Brainerd, MN USA
Date of Production: March 2013
Run Number: 19588

Printed and bound in the United States.
BG 10 9 8 7 6 5 4 3 2 1

For Warren, with thanks for the map of seventeenth-century Rome.

July 5

HOME, SWEET ROME

Even with all the high-tech ways of communicating, nothing compares to actual physical mail delivered the old-fashioned way by a real person. Getting a letter was always special, but even better was getting one at a hotel. Better still, at a hotel in Paris. That made the postcard even more romantic and exotic. But what made it the most mysterious was that it was from Mom.

She'd vanished more than six months ago, and for most of that time we hadn't heard a word from her. At first, my older brother, Malcolm, was sure she'd run off with some guy. Dad insisted she was on some super-important business trip. I didn't know what to think. But after weeks of being scared she'd been murdered, then furious that she'd simply left, now we knew the truth.

Mom was a time traveler. She was stuck somewhere in the

past trying to change some event so that something terrible wouldn't happen to us in the future.

That was unbelievable fact number one. Except that Dad knew all about her time traveling. He simply hadn't brought it up because he thought Mom's time-traveling days were long over. So when she disappeared, he didn't immediately think, "Oh, she's in the past somewhere. She'll be home for dinner before you know it." But after a while, he began to suspect some weird time-travel stuff was happening.

It would have been nice if he'd said something to us then instead of letting us find out the hard way that Mom could time-travel. Seems like something you should share with your kids, like an earlier marriage or a half sibling, not something to be kept secret.

Unbelievable fact number two was that I could time-travel, too, which was how I bumped into Mom in nineteenth-century Paris and discovered the truth. If I touched the right thing (Mom called them touchstones), I'd be whirled into the past. The first time it happened was at the top of Notre Dame cathedral, and believe me, I wasn't trying to go anywhere. I touched one of the gargoyles perched on the edge of the railing, and before I knew it, the city below me had changed completely. No more cars or buses, no more satellite dishes, just horses and buggies like in a movie about the 1800s.

So even though we'd been in Paris for almost a week, I'd

spent most of that time not really here but in the past, trying to follow Mom's directions so we could go back to being a normal family. Dad and Malcolm couldn't time-travel (at least not as far as we knew), but they helped me by doing research and figuring out what I should be changing and how. We actually made a pretty good team.

For all my time (yes, pun intended) with famous artists and writers like Degas and Zola, I had only halfway changed anything in the past. I wasn't a total failure, but I wasn't a huge success, either. Mom had left me cryptic notes in the nineteenth century that hinted I would have more to do. The postcard here and now probably had some kind of instructions.

Since we'd been busy most of the week in Paris trying to right a horrible wrong in history, we'd had only a few hours to play tourist. Last night, Dad, Malcolm, and I ate dinner outside at a cute little brasserie and walked back to our hotel in the warm summer night, just like your average American sightseers.

"I love this!" Malcolm had said, flinging his arms wide as we strolled down the narrow streets of the Marais. "We should be homeschooled for all of high school, just traveling from one amazing city to another!"

"At least for this year," Dad agreed. "While I have this grant. And until we get Mom back where she belongs."

I guess I should mention that Dad is a photographer. And

that grant was the excuse he had needed to take us all over the place while he took pictures of the Wonders of the World. Not the original seven wonders, but ones the ancient Greeks didn't know about, like the Golden Gate Bridge or the Eiffel Tower. Really he was trying to track down Mom. We all were.

So when the postcard was delivered to our breakfast table along with the basket of croissants this morning, Dad almost jumped out of his chair.

"It's from Mom! She's telling us where we need to go next."

One side showed the Colosseum in Rome. On the other side was a message.

Dear David, Malcolm, and Mira,

I wish I could write more, but I don't have much time. (The one thing you'd think I'd have plenty of!) All I can say is that Mira's next time travel will be trickier because she'll need to disguise herself as a boy. And before she finds a touchstone, she needs to eat some ragwort. This is essential—you must not forget the ragwort. But not too much since it can be poisonous.

Please hurry! I miss you all terribly!

Love,
Mom

Mom sounded scared. Her handwriting looked rushed and panicked. Which, of course, made me scared. And she acted like I could pick how and when I time-traveled. So far it seemed like a complete accident. I stumbled onto touchstones or I didn't. I couldn't plan anything.

"Sounds like she's in some kind of trouble." Dad flipped the postcard over, staring at the picture side. "In Rome."

"But what am I supposed to do there?"

"You'll figure it out once you get there. Maybe you'll get to see her!"

Dad knew that wasn't likely. There were rules to time-traveling. We weren't supposed to change anything, just observe—though Mom was breaking that rule. Despite

5

flouting the absolutely most important of all the restrictions, she seemed determined to follow the other less-important rules, like not taking anything from the past back with us. And families shouldn't time-travel together as that increased the risk that something bad would happen to change their future. As opposed to the good thing Mom wanted to happen to alter our future.

"At least Mom's telling you how to prepare this time," Malcolm said. "You can borrow my clothes and we'll figure out the ragwort thing."

"I don't understand why she's telling me how to dress. Last time my clothes changed all by themselves without me doing anything. I thought that was just part of time travel." I ran my fingers through my curly hair, which just brushed the tops of my shoulders. Should I cut it to look like a boy? Would a baggy shirt be enough to disguise any evidence of being a girl? "And what kind of mother tells her kid to eat poison?" I threw down the rest of my croissant. Suddenly it tasted like cardboard. Mom had to be really terrified to tell me to do that.

"So, we're going to Rome?" Malcolm did one of his little happy dances, jiggling in his chair. They were cute in our home movies when he was six or seven. Now that he's sixteen, they're just plain dorky. But if he wasn't worried, then maybe things weren't that bad. Maybe I was imagining that Mom was scared because I was.

"You're not worried about Mom?" I asked, hoping he would reassure me.

"Of course I am!" Malcolm said. "But I'm still glad we're going to Rome! I'll get to see the things I've read about in Pliny, Suetonius, and Livy, all that juicy ancient history." My brother was a big history buff, and I bet he knew more about that kind of stuff than his teachers did. I had to admit I was eager to see Rome, too. *Roman Holiday* was one of my favorite movies. And I was a big fan of pizza and pasta. Maybe this would be fun, not scary.

"Let's look into this ragwort thing," Dad said. He didn't seem worried or excited. Just practical. "If we can figure out why Mom told you to eat it, maybe we'll know what you're supposed to do once you go back in time."

So before we got on the overnight train for Rome, we looked up ragwort on the Internet. It didn't have any magical powers. In fact, it was very common—a weed you could find everywhere, kind of like dandelions. It even grew in a park next to the Paris train station. Suspiciously convenient. For a minute, I wondered if Mom had time-traveled to plant it just for me.

The signs said not to walk on the grass.

"Let me pick it!" Malcolm begged, not because he was eager to harvest ragwort, but because he loved the idea of ignoring the officious French warnings.

Dad scanned quickly for any police and nodded. "Hurry up!"

Malcolm stepped across the lawn in an exaggerated tiptoe, like a rubber-legged cartoon character. He picked the plant in slow motion, then pirouetted his way back to the safety of the sidewalk. Which shows how law-abiding my brother is, since this seemed like the height of bad behavior to him and he was smugly pleased with how reckless he'd been.

"Hand over the ragwort," I demanded. "And stop grinning. You act like you robbed a bank or something."

"Go ahead and eat some," Dad said. "And keep the rest in your pocket. So if you need more, you'll have it."

How would I know I needed more when I didn't even know what it was supposed to do? I nibbled on a leaf, chewed on a petal. Ick! Maybe mixed in a salad or on a sandwich, the flower would taste better. I felt like a cow grazing.

"Moo!" I joked lamely, forcing down the ragwort and waiting to feel if anything was different. "Nothing." I shrugged. "Still the same old me."

"Maybe you'll be different once we're in Rome," Malcolm offered, still proud of his great ragwort achievement.

"Maybe I'll be the same, but with a stomachache."

We boarded the train, stowed our bags, and stretched out on the hard berths. When Dad said he'd booked a sleeping car, I'd imagined something like the Orient Express in the Agatha Christie movie, an elegant train car with beds, washbasins, and closets. What we got was a cramped compartment with four bunks in it. We took up three and a gangly Swedish girl, a college student traveling during the summer break, had the fourth bed. Her English was pretty good but her strongest language was snoring. She was so loud that her nasal whistles and rumbles almost cloaked the rhythm of the wheels clacking on the tracks.

I thought I hadn't slept at all, but I must have since I woke up in the pale, thin light of dawn as the train chuffed into Termini, the main train station in Rome. Dad and Malcolm were already awake—or maybe they'd never slept. We all looked groggy and pouch-eyed. The Swedish student was still snoring, looking blissfully innocent while sounding like a tormenting demon. Even the noise we made gathering our stuff and stomping out of the compartment didn't wake her.

We stepped out into a big building full of shops, restaurants, and streams of people towing luggage. The babble of Italian, French, German, English, Russian, and other languages I didn't recognize rose over our heads. I could almost see the words floating to the ceiling like so many balloons. At the end of the train tracks, enormous boards showed all the places where passengers could be going—Paris, Geneva, Milan, Venice, Berlin, Madrid. Just reading the names, I imagined how easy it would be to get on any of those trains and find myself whisked away to someplace new and exciting.

Except we were in Rome, which was new and exciting in itself. Ever since I could hold a crayon, I've wanted to be an artist like my grandfather, and for centuries, Rome was the city where painters went to train their eye and their hand. I was here to help Mom, but I hoped I could improve my drawing while I was at it.

As soon as we walked out of the station, past the small cars and flocks of motorcycles, we saw our first ancient ruins. An enormous stone building with broad buttresses and high windows loomed across the street. It was a strange mix of styles. Later I realized they were layers, really—ancient Roman with

Renaissance doorways and modern additions. Centuries folded into one structure. Most of the building was now a museum of ancient art. Somehow the sight of that woke us all up, especially Malcolm, who launched into his history teacher mode.

"This was originally the baths of Emperor Diocletian," Malcolm explained. "Ancient Roman baths weren't just bathtubs. They were enormous spa com-plexes with gyms, warm pools, cold pools, hot pools, dressing rooms, toilets. It's so cool!" He was ready to go straight into the museum, to start exploring, but I dug in my heels.

"I'm not awake yet! I need to shower and brush my teeth." Actually, I was itching to sketch, but I felt embarrassed by my lank, unwashed hair and my sour breath. If I was a real artist, I wouldn't care. I'd just draw.

"Let's at least get a cup of coffee," Dad suggested. "Some breakfast will perk us up."

"Okay," Malcolm agreed reluctantly, even though I knew how much he depended on coffee, almost as much as Dad did, which was a lot. If my brother was an artist, he'd already be whipping out his sketchbook, caffeinated or not. Why couldn't I be more like him?

But before we came to a café, we passed a set of Renaissance doors carved out of a wall of Roman rubble, also part of the ancient baths. The plain cross nailed high above the arched entrances and the words S. MARIA DEGLI ANGELI spelled out in black tiles on a severe white band were the only signs it was a church. Malcolm stopped at the central door, pleading with his big, brown puppy eyes.

I had to smile. Only my brother would think a Roman ruin converted into a church was a special treat worth begging for.

"Just a quick look, all right?" Dad said. "We'll have plenty of chances to see things later."

"Promise—just in and out!" Malcolm pushed open the door, and the early morning sunshine disappeared into a vast, hushed space. For a church, it still felt classically ancient with colored marble panels, tall columns, and wide arches marking out the space in spare geometric symmetry. There were altarpieces and crosses in the chapels, but the big barrel vaults and the red, pink, and toffee-colored marble gave an impression of imperial grandeur, a seriousness of Roman law and order. The churchy bits seemed added on, not part of the building's heart and soul, but scraps of decoration that could easily be removed.

In such an architectural marvel, Dad couldn't help himself. Even without coffee to jump-start his brain, he pulled out his guidebook and explained that we were standing in what was once part of the baths of Emperor Diocletian and later turned into a church by Michelangelo—yes, *that* Michelangelo, the one who painted the Sistine Chapel. We'd been in Rome for maybe five minutes, and we were already seeing ancient and Renaissance Rome in the same building! That seemed like some amazing time travel right there.

We're in Rome! I thought, shivering with excitement. Somehow now it seemed real. *The Sistine Chapel is here! Plus pizza and pasta and gelato.* I wanted to go everywhere, eat everything at once. Suddenly I was starving, but something in the church kept me there. A deep crack split across the floor. As I came closer I saw it was a groove etched into the marble, zodiac symbols ranged on both sides of it.

It was some kind of calendar, and anything that measured time was magnetic for me now. I wondered if it could it be a touchstone. Could I have found one already, ready to hurl me back into time so soon? I could feel it pulsating with power, throbbing like a vein in the skin of the church. I hoped it was just the ragwort making me dizzy, or the lack of sleep, but just in case I stepped away from the bronze line.

"It's a sundial and a meridian all at once," I said, reading the

explanation on the wall of the church while keeping a safe distance from the marker.

"How do you know that?" Malcolm was suspicious.

"Don't act so shocked. Maybe I don't know about science-y stuff, but I can read a label." *I can feel the time locked inside of it*, I almost shouted, but I didn't because that would make me sound as crazy as I felt.

"That label, there?" Malcolm pointed.

"Yeah?" I raised an eyebrow. Did he think I'd forgotten how to read now? Or could he somehow see the way the meridian was tugging at me, drawing me to it the way a river current carries along a leaf?

"Since when do you know Italian?" he asked.

"Since never. I don't." So he couldn't feel the meridian's pull. He just thought I was showing off.

"Then how come you're reading an explanation written in Italian?"

I looked at the sign again. I'd just read it without thinking, but now that Malcolm mentioned it, I saw that, yes, it was in Italian, and yes, I could still understand it.

I gaped at Malcolm. "I can read Italian!" I hurried over to a cluster of tourists. Could I understand what they were saying? The pink-faced man and his equally pink wife and children sounded like they were eating meatballs, not speaking Italian. I listened for a while, until the father glared at me like I was an annoying beggar. Anyway,

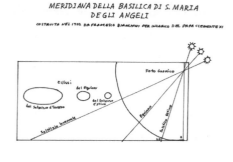

the guttural words were German or Swedish, and I didn't understand anything. Maybe ragwort was specific in its language ability.

Next, I attached myself to a cluster of tourists listening to a tall, skinny man dressed like an undertaker and lecturing about the painting over the main altar. The elegantly dressed woman in front of me turned around and said something that didn't sound friendly at all. She was speaking French far too rapidly for me to follow, but I gathered that she thought I was freeloading off their tour.

I scurried away, sitting in a pew next to two blond teenage girls who were laughing together as if they were in a park, not a church. I thought I'd hear some juicy gossip, but all I gleaned were some Russian-sounding words and a suspicious look from one of the girls. I got up, exasperated and embarrassed. Didn't any Italians tour Italy? Didn't Florentines visit Rome? Maybe someone from Venice or Milan?

Then I saw an old man hobbling next to his wife. They both looked far too old to travel much. I inched closer, trying to look nonchalant like just another tourist. Luckily, they didn't notice me at all. They were speaking Italian, discussing what to eat for lunch and whether their daughter would drop by later. I could understand it all!

I rushed back to Malcolm and Dad.

"What was that about?" my brother asked. "You just ran away, all wild-eyed. Were you bugging that family? Spying on that tour group? Harassing that old couple?"

"I can understand Italian!" I said, excited. "Speaking, reading, everything! Isn't that amazing!"

"That's why Mom wanted you to eat the ragwort! It's the only explanation! Here, let me try." Malcolm held out his hand eagerly. That was a rare sight—my brother begging to eat something green.

I gave Malcolm a leaf and a petal since I wasn't sure what part of the plant worked. He grimaced at the taste, swallowing quickly. But when he tried to read the sign, it was still indecipherable to him.

"Maybe it needs more time to work," I suggested.

"Or maybe it only works if you have the time-travel gene, which obviously I don't. It's so unfair! Not only do you get to see all these cool historical things, but you get instant languages!"

I grinned. I hadn't felt that lucky about time-traveling, but the language thing was definitely a plus.

"What time do you think I'll travel to?" I asked, changing the subject to make Malcolm feel better. Which was clumsy of me since he was as jealous of time-traveling as he was of instant language skills.

Malcolm arched an eyebrow. He saw right through my lame attempt. "If you're lucky, you'll see Michelangelo paint the Sistine Chapel. Or better yet, you'll watch gladiators fight it out in the Colosseum!"

"You're not time-traveling yet," Dad said. "Let's enjoy the city. But first we should check into our hotel. I found us a place near the train station, so it can't be far."

I agreed. I wanted to explore Rome, the modern city, before I got hurled into the past. But the pull of the meridian was stronger now, like a mesmerizing magnet. I paced alongside it, measuring the seasons with my footsteps. I clenched my hands tightly to keep from touching anything, focusing on the floor with its etched designs for each sign of the zodiac. I looked up and Malcolm was right next to me, reassuring in his familiar lankiness and thick dark curls.

"Are you okay?" he asked. "You're pale and sweaty."

"I'm just tired, that's all," I said, relieved to be near him. I grabbed his arm, pushing him between myself and the meridian. I needed him to shield me from it or I wouldn't be able to stop myself. I'd touch it.

"What's wrong with you?" Malcolm shook himself free. "You look like you're going to puke!"

I bent over, feeling sick. It was stronger than me. I couldn't resist anymore. Something, some force, yanked my hand down, thrusting my fingers toward the archer, Sagittarius.

The marble floor melted under my hand, rippling like waves. The high arched walls fell away, the great dome spun off, and a black, starry sky swept around me, pulling me into a dizzying vortex. "*No!*" I screamed, but my words were caught in the ripples of time, cast out on the currents of centuries.

winter?

When the world steadied around me and my legs stopped trembling, I was back in Santa Maria degli Angeli, but the meridian was gone. So were the tourists, my dad, and Malcolm. The church was empty and cold. I guessed it must be winter and the thick stone walls kept in the chill like an enormous refrigerator.

I was dressed in a loose white shirt, belted at the waist with some kind of leather vest over it, as well as pants, thick stockings, and leather boots. A hat with a feather perched on my head, my hair still shoulder-length, and a heavy woolen cloak draped over my shoulders. Boy clothes, I assumed, since I wasn't wearing long, heavy skirts. I reached into the pocket sewn inside my vest and found the ragwort and my sketchbook. At least I had those things still with me.

I had thought the church was empty, but now I noticed a

heavy figure sitting in a back pew. A monk wearing brown robes with the hood pulled up. His back was to me, so luckily he didn't see me suddenly appear out of nowhere. If that ever happened, would I be burned at the stake for witchcraft? Those were the kind of time-travel rules I needed to know— how to escape in emergencies, how to find a touchstone when necessary.

All I knew was that, according to Mom, if I traveled to a certain time and place, there had to be a reason. My job was to figure out what I needed to do and do it. I wanted to find Mom and bring her back with me, but I had no idea how. The only thing I knew for sure was that until something in the past was changed the way she wanted it to be, she wouldn't come home.

I hadn't spent enough time in modern Rome to have any sense of how the city was laid out. Where was I supposed to go? What was I supposed to do? When Malcolm, Dad, and I had entered, there'd been a big plaza in front of the church with a fountain in the middle, ringed by a traffic circle swarming with buses and cars. Once I stepped outside, I found all that had vanished and in its place stood a facade of ruined porticos, part of the ancient baths. Beyond that stretched fields stubbled with broken columns and bits of sculpture. Where had the city gone?

My stomach pitched and a

shiver ran up my neck. Was this the time of the barbarian invasion when Rome was sacked? Or the time when the whole city burned while the emperor Nero played his violin? I didn't know enough history to be sure, and to be honest, the whole story of Nero fiddling while Rome burned was something I only knew from cartoons.

A hand gripped my elbow and I whipped around, trying to wrench myself free.

"Mira!" a voice hissed. "It's me! Calm down and come with me." I had no idea who "me" was, but I found myself facing the monk from the church. His hood shadowed his face so I couldn't make out his features, but clearly he knew who I was.

"Your mother told me to look out for you."

Now I recognized the voice! It was the walrus-moustache man, Morton, the fellow time traveler I had met in nineteenth-century Paris, the one who said he was Mom's friend. He'd explained to me what she wanted me to do when we were in Paris. I hoped he would do the same now.

"You ate the ragwort, right?" Morton asked.

"Yes! Is that why I can understand Italian?"

"Exactly! And you have the right clothes on, so let's get you to Del Monte's."

"I'm going to a ketchup factory? Or making fruit cocktail? What am I supposed to do? Is Mom okay?"

"Your mother is fine. Though I wish she'd explain things more clearly to you so I wouldn't have to."

"Me, too, but she hasn't, so tell me something!"

Morton shrugged. "All I know is that she's working inside the Vatican, trying to convince the Pope of something. But she must have gotten a message to you since you're wearing the right clothes."

"I didn't pick the clothes. They picked me. They just happened, same as the touchstone. I don't have control over any of this."

Morton shook his head as he led me down the broad dirt road crossing the fields. "You have more control than you think. Maybe not consciously yet, but that'll come with time. Time, hah!" He snorted as if he'd made an incredibly clever pun—time, time travel, get it? But I wasn't laughing. I was as confused as ever.

"What happened to the city?" I asked. "When is it?"

"We're still in Rome, but this is the outskirts of the city in the sixteenth century."

"The sixteenth century?" I gasped. It wasn't the time of barbarian hordes or gladiators, but it was way far back in the past. Would I be able to fit in?

We turned onto a wider road rutted by cart wheels. Ahead of

us, a shepherd drove a flock of goats across the way. We could have been in the middle of the countryside, not near a great city.

"Where are we going?"

"I promised your mother I'd take you to Del Monte's palazzo, and that's what I'm doing." A cart pulled by oxen rumbled toward us, followed by a group of monks, clashing with the sudden image I'd had of cans of fruit stacked in a tall tower.

"Am I going to some kind of factory? What does Mom want me to change this time?"

"She can explain all that."

"But you know the rules! We can't be together at the same time in the past. She'll be doing everything she can to avoid me."

"She'll get information to you like she did in Paris. She's here at the papal palace. This is getting too dangerous for me." The monk looked nervously over his shoulder even though nobody was near us.

"Why? Because we're trying to change the past and we're not supposed to?"

"*Shhh!*" Morton jerked my arm angrily. "Do you want to get arrested?"

I didn't see any police, but then how would I know if I did? What did a sixteenth-century Roman policeman look like? Did police even exist then? Narrow dirt streets branched off the road now, lined with houses and vegetable gardens, small orchards and stone barns. At first there were only a few people, but soon the lanes were crowded with donkey carts, peddlers, monks, soldiers with cloaks and swords, mangy dogs, and grubby children.

The people were dressed as if they'd stepped out of an old painting. The women wore long skirts with scarves over their heads and around their shoulders, while the men wore tunics and leggings, blouses, and tight pants with boots. The poor people wore scratchy-looking clothes in grays, browns, and blacks, while the wealthier ones sported rich colors, as if even blues, yellows, and reds were reserved for finer folk. I was dressed in between the two. No fancy materials or colors, but I did have a nice hat—with a feather, even—and there were no holes or stains anywhere.

The air was no longer fresh with the wintry scent of grass. Instead it was heavy with sweat, smoke, rotten vegetables, and the nasty bathroom smells that are reserved for tunnels and alleys in modern cities, but in this time filled even the busy, main streets. If the weather weren't so crisp and cool, the stench would have been suffocating. I'd hate to travel back to this time in the summer.

I stood there frozen with doubt, while unshaven, unwashed people jostled around me. I'd had no idea what great inventions soap and shampoo were!

"I don't mean the Roman police!" Morton said. He must have

thought I'd stopped because I was searching for one, not because I wasn't sure how to breathe safely in sixteenth-century Rome. "See that fellow over there—the nasty-looking one in the red cloak with a hood? That's a *sbirro*, a cop. He won't bother you. I'm talking about the Watchers."

A chill ran through me, and suddenly the stench didn't matter at all. "You mean there are time-travel police to enforce those rules Mom told me?"

"Yes! And you and your mom are breaking the most important one!"

"I don't mean to put you in danger, and I'm grateful for all your help, really I am." I tried to sound determined and brave, somebody worthy of being helped, someone reliable. "But since you're already taking a risk, can you please tell me more, explain what I need to do here?"

"I'm sorry," he said, and he actually did look regretful. "I just can't. That's really for your mother to do."

Or for me to figure out on my own.

The narrow streets opened onto a piazza. In the center, an ancient Roman column towered over us, with images winding up it like a carved comic strip. Soldiers marched with spears rayed out from their shoulders; boats surged on stone waves;

and horses pulled chariots of helmeted men. I couldn't help but stop and stare, forgetting about Mom, Morton, the Watchers, everything except this incredible sculpture. Part of me was in awe, part of me was just plain jealous. If only I had that kind of talent!

This was the good part of time travel—seeing amazing things like this before they were ruined by being next door to a fast-food place or junked up with modern billboards or totally destroyed to make way for a parking lot. I wondered if the column would still be standing when I got back to modern Rome. An old temple stood behind the column, weeds growing out of it. Once, priests would have offered burnt sacrifices there, but now goats scampered down the steps. It was strange to see something so beautiful being treated so shabbily.

"Remember the woman in Paris who took my note from the cathedral? The one waiting for your mother?" Morton was already leading us across the piazza and then ducking down yet another narrow side street.

How could I forget? The woman had tried to attack Mom, had chased me through the streets, and was probably responsible for the murder of Émile Zola, the writer Mom and I both knew. The woman was more than creepy! And now I understood why she'd said my mother was the one who was doing the wrong thing, not her. She had to be a Watcher!

What had she called herself? Madame Le-something-or-other? What would she call herself here, I wondered. It didn't matter; I was sure I'd recognize her. She was stunningly beautiful with wide violet eyes in a creamy oval face, a serene brow, and a strong chin. Even dressed like a man, she'd be gorgeous.

"Have you seen her? Is she here?"

"Not that I know, but she's smart. She'll figure things out. She always does." Morton grabbed my arm again, and I trotted to keep up with his brisk pace. For someone so waddly and awkward, he managed quite a clip. He wanted to deliver me to Del Monte's and be done with me. Which meant I had to pump him for information while I had him. If the Watcher was after both him and Mom, that seemed like a sign to believe whatever he said.

"First of all, when exactly is it now? And what's Del Monte's and what do I need to do there?"

"The date is 23 March, 1595. And Del Monte is a who, not a what. He's a cardinal, very influential, very important. Many people want him to become Pope, but even without that title, he has a lot of political clout."

I tried to remember what happened in 1595 that might be important. The closest date I could think of was 1492 when Columbus sailed the ocean blue. After that came 1776 when the Declaration of Independence was signed. Between those two dates was the Mayflower landing on Plymouth Rock, but that didn't matter in Italy. I needed a better sense of world history.

Italy, the 1500s—of course! That was the Renaissance, when Michelangelo, Leonardo da Vinci, and Galileo were alive. Would I get to meet Michelangelo like Malcolm had thought? My stomach fluttered with excitement.

"Del Monte has connections with the powerful Medici family in Florence. He represents their interests to the Vatican, to the Pope, I mean. And he's the patron of a very important painter."

Finally, a familiar name! I'd heard of the Medici family. They were rich bankers who ran the city of Florence during the Renaissance. Michelangelo did some sculpture for them. And hadn't a pope commissioned him to paint the Sistine Chapel? Maybe I was supposed to help Michelangelo!

"Mira, are you listening?" Morton shook my arm as we snaked our way down a narrow street pocked with smelly piles I definitely didn't want to step in.

"I heard you," I said. "An important painter. Michelangelo?"

"Exactly! Your mother wants you to act as a servant in the household and listen to what's happening. Something to do with the Inquisition, something horrible."

The Inquisition? I pictured medieval torture devices like the rack or the iron maiden. What was Mom getting involved with? I shivered in the late afternoon chill. As long as I didn't have to go into any dark dungeons, I could do this, I told myself. I would figure out what to do.

The lane spilled us out into the shallow bowl of a piazza. The sun was low in the sky, but the golden light lit up an ancient temple on our left, erasing all thoughts of dank prisons with its sheer beauty. Unlike the temple we'd passed before, this one was crowned with a wide dome, which seemed to lift the whole building up into the sky. Large letters were incised above the entrance in an elegant script: M. AGRIPPA L.F.COS. TERTIUM. FECIT.

The columns along the front had a dignified rhythm. The proportions of each element were all perfect, giving the sense of absolute measure. If you could build logic, reason, stability, peace—that's what it would look like. Just seeing it made me feel whole, complete.

"What do the words mean?" I asked.

"I'm not a tour guide!" Morton snapped.

I must have looked as taken aback as I felt, because he apologized and ushered us inside, where the beautifully proportioned space held us like we were floating in a bubble.

"This is the Pantheon. It was built as a temple to all the Roman gods by Marcus Agrippa, a general under the emperor Augustus in the first century BC. That's what's written outside: 'Marcus Agrippa, son of Lucius, having been consul three times, built it.' Now it's a church and some of the most famous Italians in history are buried here, like the painter Raphael."

"Now on to Del Monte's," Morton said, as I tipped back my head, watching the clouds across the opening in the dome, like the eye of heaven looking down on human measure. The same rhythmic cadence of the columns outside marched up the dome in the elegant coffering. The lines of the architecture were even crisper in contrast to the puffy clouds revealed by the hole.

"I'm not sure I'm ready," I said, drinking in the peacefulness.

"Ready or not, there you go! I can't stay any longer. I really can't!" He was getting edgier by the minute. You'd think the serenity of such a perfect space would calm him down, but the magic of the Pantheon was wasted on him.

The sun was setting as we dived

back into the crowded streets. Now I understood why Morton was in a hurry. There were no streetlights and it didn't seem safe to be outside after dark in a strange city in a strange time.

Morton pulled me into the doorway of a big building facing a church. "This isn't the front door, of course. I'm taking you to the servants' entrance. I've arranged for you to work in the kitchen here."

"What am I supposed to do?"

"Fetch firewood, chop onions, I don't know! Whatever they tell you to do. The important thing is that you keep your ears open. Your mother will be in touch. She always figures out a way."

"And what about the woman, the Watcher?"

"She'll figure out a way, too, I'm sure, so beware!"

"That's the best advice you can give me?"

Morton's face sagged. "I'm trying to help you, Mira, but this is all I can do. Good luck!" He pulled his hood down over his face, strode back to the front of the church we'd just passed, and reached out to touch the statue by the door. The air around him thickened as swirling clouds of purple and yellow smoke sucked him up into a strange tornado. There was a loud popping sound and the clouds were gone. The monk had vanished. And with him, the only connection to my mother.

I shivered in the doorway, not sure what to do. I could try touching the statue, too, hoping the touchstone would work a second time, and be back safe with Dad and Malcolm. I shook my head. I had a job to do. I squared my shoulders, trying to feel brave, and knocked on the door. I held my hat in my nervous fingers, trying to look like an ordinary servant boy reporting for kitchen duty.

Nobody answered so I knocked again. Now that the choice of entering or not had been taken away from me, I was frantic to get in. I picked up a stone and pounded it on the door. Somebody had to hear me now!

"*Basta!*" a deep voice growled behind the door. "I'm coming, I'm coming!" The door scraped open, and a short, thick man with caterpillar eyebrows and a potato nose scowled at me. He was wearing clothes a lot like mine, except ten sizes bigger, and was holding a chicken upside down by the legs.

A live chicken, wings flapping and everything.

"Yes?" the man demanded.

Somehow the sight of the chicken unnerved me more than anything else that had happened so far. "I'm sorry to disturb you," I finally managed to stammer. At least I was speaking Italian. That was something to be relieved about.

32

"Then why did you?" barked the man.

It was the chicken. Or it was the man yelling. Or it was both, but I made a stupid mistake. "I'm Mira," I mumbled, then realized what I'd done. "Marco, I mean!" I shouted, trying to erase my words. "I'm the new servant. For the kitchen. For Del Monte. Marco!" I repeated the name loudly.

"Finally! Thought you'd never get here!" I was relieved that the man hadn't heard my real name. Then he thrust the chicken at me. "You can start with tonight's supper." And there went any relief I'd felt.

I'm sure I turned six shades paler. I certainly felt faint. I'd helped Dad barbecue a chicken. I'd breaded and fried chicken parts with Mom. But the first ingredient was always a cut-up chicken, plucked and wrapped in plastic. With no feathers, no feet, and definitely no head with beady eyes staring at me.

I shook my head. "Not that kind of servant," I mumbled. "I can get firewood." Though I had no idea how to do that, either. At least I wouldn't have to kill anything.

"You're the kind of servant I say you are if you want a place here!" the man roared, showing off his rotten yellow teeth and the rancid gaps between them. He shoved the chicken in my face, and as it squawked and squirmed, I did the unthinkable—I grabbed it by the legs and held it out from me.

"Good!" the man approved. "Now get busy!" He shoved me down the hall into a cavernous kitchen. An enormous table was filled with crockery, piles of onions, heaps of carrots, big round loaves of bread stacked up like wheels, cheeses, herbs, and one dead rabbit.

I shivered, thinking my chicken would soon be joining the rabbit corpse.

"When you're done, Giovanni here will show you around." The man pointed to a boy about my age with golden hair and a sweet smile. He looked at me and nodded, and I felt a jolt of recognition. I knew him, knew him well. He was so familiar—something in his eyes, in the curve of his full lips. But how could I possibly know him unless he was a time traveler, too?

The stout man was done with me. He strode out of the room through a door at the other end. I could hear his footsteps echoing as he stomped upstairs. I just stood there stunned and awkward, holding the squawking chicken, staring at the dead rabbit.

Giovanni took the chicken from me without a word and snapped its neck so quickly that I didn't realize what he was doing until it was over. The chicken lay on the table now with its neck broken. I actually felt sorry for it.

"Seemed like you needed some help," he said. "But I suppose you can pluck the bird yourself, can't you?"

His voice was even more familiar than the rest of him. I closed my eyes, trying to remember how I knew him, who he was.

"You can pluck a chicken?" he asked again.

"Um," I answered. "Not really, no. Maybe I could do something else instead?"

Giovanni sighed loudly, grabbed the chicken, sat on a stool with the bird between his knees, and started pulling out feathers so quickly I could barely follow his fingers.

"I'm sorry I'm so useless," I said. "Tell me what to do and I'll do it."

"You can pluck a chicken," Giovanni said deadpan. "Oh, wait, you can't. Why are you working in a kitchen then?"

"I don't know." I sighed. "My uncle got me this place. He figured I'd learn on the job."

"So do you want to learn how to pluck a chicken?" he asked, the chicken already half naked under his flying fingers.

"Not really," I said. "I'd rather chop stuff or fetch water or wash dishes."

"You can't really pick and choose, you know," Giovanni said. "You're a strange fellow. I can't place your accent. Where are you from?"

If I was pale before, now I turned totally white. I hadn't prepared any kind of cover story. And Morton hadn't helped with any ideas. I knew I was speaking Italian, but I had no idea what kind of accent I had, where I should say I was from. I said the first Italian town I could think of.

"No place you've heard of, a tiny village near Venice."

"Ah, the Veneto! I've heard that Venice is a magical city, beautiful with all its canals. My master's been to Venice. Not me."

"Your master? Del Monte?"

"Monsignore Del Monte, of course, he was born there, but no, he's not my master. Michelangelo Merisi da Caravaggio is my master. He's a painter, a great artist."

That had to be the Michelangelo Morton meant—not the Florentine sculptor. I felt a pang of disappointment. No Sistine Chapel for me. No famous genius. I still had to figure out what I was supposed to do here. Maybe this other painter was a clue.

"If Caravaggio's your master, why are you in the kitchen preparing a chicken?"

By now the chicken was all pimply skin, not a single feather left.

"As a favor to you, the new boy. I was new once myself. I know how that feels. And I can show you around, as Carlo, the cook, asked. But you'll have to do better with the chicken next time. I'm usually not in the kitchen." Giovanni winked and my heart started thudding.

I followed him up the back staircase all the way to the top floor. He pushed open a door and showed me a small, spare room with a narrow bed, a crucifix nailed to the wall over it, and nothing else.

"I sleep here," he said. "I'm guessing you'll sleep in the kitchen, warmer that way."

"There's no room for me up here?" I asked. Sleeping in a kitchen sounded one step up from sleeping in a barn. I pointed to a door down the hall.

"Other servants sleep there. In the morning I'll show you where my master works. It's too dark now to see anything."

We wound our way back down the stairs. The kitchen was bustling now with dinner preparations. The chicken had vanished. Into a pot, probably. The rabbit was gone, too. Probably in another pot. The table was still laden with carrots and onions, now being chopped by the beefy Carlo.

"Ah, there you are!" Carlo waved his big knife at me. "Worthless bag of bones! This is your work, not mine!"

"I'm sorry," I stammered, taking the knife and starting in on some carrots. At least chopping vegetables was something familiar. How would I pull this off? It was all too strange and I didn't know the right kind of things. What use was it to know how to make mac and cheese from a box when I couldn't kill and pluck a chicken? I could zap food in a microwave but not gut a pig. I hoped tomorrow's dinner wouldn't be pork chops.

"I'll help," Giovanni offered, picking up another knife and slicing the onions.

"Thank you," I whispered. I was so relieved that he was there, someone I could trust, a strangely familiar face, even if I couldn't remember what the connection was.

"I know what it's like when you first come to Rome. Such

37

a big city, so many people, so much noise, so many smells! I came from a small village outside Udine. My uncle brought me here because he was setting up a tavern. When I first saw St. Peter's, I nearly fell over! I'd never seen anything so grand. When I walked inside, I felt like I was Jonah, swallowed by the whale. I could feel the stones of the church breathing around me." Giovanni looked up at me shyly. "I don't know why I'm telling you this. You'll think I'm crazy."

I smiled. "No, I know just what you mean." I'd felt something similar in Notre Dame cathedral. "Could you take me to St. Peter's, show me around the city a bit?" I held my breath, waiting for his answer. This would be so much easier, so much less lonely with him as a friend.

"Of course." Giovanni nodded. "When my master doesn't need me—and yours doesn't need you. Caravaggio spends long hours painting, so unless he sends me for colors or brushes, my time is my own. The evenings are when he wants me most, or when he goes to see patrons, important men interested in buying his pictures."

"Giovanni!" A deep voice roared down the stairs.

"That's him now. I'll see you in the morning." Giovanni winked. And I was left alone, chopping onions, tears streaming down my face.

Somehow I made it through that first night with only a slight cut on my thumb. Carlo yelled and bellowed and screamed constantly. Nothing I did was right, but I managed to get the chicken cooked with only a little bit of it burned. If only the main course had been spaghetti, it would have been so much easier! I was bone-tired and sick of being yelled at by the time we were through, and I could finally huddle over my own meager bowl of beans.

When I fell asleep on the hard bench by the warm hearth, all I could think of was how grateful I was to only be a visitor, to know I didn't belong here. Though at least, I had to admit, it was quiet. No roar of traffic, no early-morning garbage trucks. And no snoring since, luckily for me, Carlo slept upstairs near Giovanni.

In the morning, more yelling from Carlo—heat the water, boil the coffee, slice the bread, stoke the fire, fetch more wood. I felt like Cinderella, only with no hope of a prince. At least I didn't have to kill anything, but by the time Giovanni came down to the kitchen, I'd been working for hours and done absolutely nothing useful.

How was I supposed to help Mom if I was chained to a kitchen? Could I have imagined better clothing for myself, something noble and rich looking? Morton said I had control over what I ended up wearing, but I had no idea how to make anything happen, much less choose a wardrobe.

Carlo had left for the market and I was sweeping the floor when Giovanni came down.

"Good morning!" He beamed that angelic smile at me. "How was your first night here?"

"Not bad," I admitted. "It was warm, like you said it would be."

"Come, I want to show you something!" Giovanni grabbed a hunk of bread and started chewing as he led me back up the stairs to the servants' quarters. This time he opened the door to a big, open room with golden morning light streaming in through the tall windows. The ceiling was high enough to allow an enormous canvas to stand against one wall.

A heavy easel held another painting, this one almost finished. A shield and sword leaned against a leather chest in one corner, like props in a play. A board set on barrels held pots of pigment, brushes, and an old painting that had blobs of color on it as if somebody was using it as a palette. It was a real artist's studio, the kind I dreamed I'd have one day.

I held my breath as I looked at the picture on the easel. It showed Mary, Joseph, and the baby Jesus. On the right half of the painting, Mary sat holding her son, her weary chin resting lightly on the baby's head.

I'd seen a lot of baby Jesuses in all the museums Mom and Dad dragged us to, and usually they looked like miniature adults with peanut heads or like big, chunky salami babies.

They never looked like real children. Except this baby. I could imagine touching the soft, doughy skin, the wispy curls of silky hair. I could almost feel the baby's weight in Mary's arms. How did the artist do that, I wondered. How could paint on a canvas come to life that way? Could I ever paint half as well?

Joseph sat on the other side of the picture, holding up a book of music. He looked like somebody I'd passed in the street yesterday, just a regular Roman guy. But the figure that took my breath away was the angel standing between Joseph and Mary. His back was to the viewer as he played his violin, reading the score that Joseph held up for him. A white cloth circled his waist and billowed around his legs, as if he'd just flown down to earth and the wind was still whipping the fabric.

From his back sprouted a magnificent pair of dove-gray wings, the feathers looking so real that I could imagine their soft touch. With his head tilted in profile, his golden curls still settling from his winged descent, the angel was completely recognizable—it was Giovanni! I smiled, thinking that Caravaggio saw his servant as an angel just as I did.

"*Bello*, no?" Giovanni said. He was proud of his image and not at all embarrassed by his near-nakedness.

"It's incredible!" I breathed. Not only because of the handsome angel and the believable baby, but because each texture felt so right and true—from the liquid eye of the donkey nosing his way over Joseph's shoulder to the wicker cask around the wine bottle, the shiny stones on the ground, the rustling leaves in the tree. It was a vision of reality that was better than real, the way only art can make it.

Before I could look around at the other pictures, the door swung open and a man stomped in wearing a black cloak over a red velvet tunic. The clothes were of fine quality, unlike mine, but they were dirty, stained, even torn in places. The man wearing them was young, only a little older than Giovanni or my brother, Malcolm, but he carried himself with a masterful swagger. His dark eyes were expressive, warm, and strikingly honest, but there was bravado in his gestures.

"Maestro," Giovanni said. "This is my friend Marco from the Veneto. He's working in the kitchen, but it doesn't agree with him. Perhaps you could hire him?"

I didn't know what to say. Working for an artist beat killing chickens any day!

"Marco, eh?" Caravaggio said, stroking his chin and examining me.

What if he wanted to paint me? I gulped. No way I could pose the way Giovanni had, bare except for a fluttering cloth. Maybe the kitchen was better after all.

"I'm sure I can find something for you to do, at least for a month or so. Can you read and write?"

"I can," I said. Giovanni looked surprised by my answer. Maybe I had some valuable skills after all.

"Latin?" Caravaggio persisted.

I wondered how much language skill the ragwort had given me. No German or French, I knew that. But really, how different could Latin be from Italian? If I understood one, I bet I could manage the other, so I nodded yes.

"Then really you should be working for Del Monte. I know he's looking for someone to help him catalog his books and copy out reports and letters for his archives. I'll make the introduction, and he's sure to take you on."

This had to be what Mom wanted! I couldn't change the past from the kitchen, but I might be able to by Del Monte's side. At least I'd be in a position to learn more about church business, including the Inquisition.

"Thank you, sir," I said. "I'm very grateful." I gestured toward the easel. "And I'm much impressed by your painting. It's so vivid, so real. I've never seen anything like it."

Caravaggio smiled. For a moment he looked like a sweet, young boy. "Nobody has! This is a new kind of painting, drawing from real life, not from some ideal models that exist only in ancient sculpture or in artists' sketchbooks."

He was a strange mix of pride and plain speaking. Normally, I'd think someone who talked like that was full of himself, but he was so matter-of-fact. And truly talented. I liked him right away, so much that a tiny sliver of me wanted to show him my own drawings, prove to him that I was a fellow artist. But I was kidding myself. He was way out of my league.

Caravaggio picked up a circular painting that looked like a shield. "This is one I just finished for Del Monte. He wanted it as a gift for the Medici ruler of Florence."

The shield was decorated with the decapitated head of

Medusa, eyes and mouth grimacing in a horror that seemed very much alive. Snakes writhed vigorously from her head. They didn't seem dead, either. Only the blood spurting from the neck proved the monster had been vanquished.

"If I remember my mythology correctly, the Greek hero Jason killed Medusa by seeing her reflection in his shiny shield, since if he'd looked at her directly, he would have been turned to stone." I tried to sound impressive, worthy of working for Del Monte.

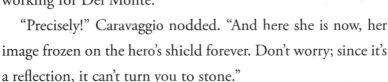

"Precisely!" Caravaggio nodded. "And here she is now, her image frozen on the hero's shield forever. Don't worry; since it's a reflection, it can't turn you to stone."

"That's very clever," I said, struck by how a reflection in a mirror and a painted reflection were both versions of the real thing, both shadows of the truth. As I stared, gripped by the horror on the face, a realization flooded me. I turned to Caravaggio, appalled. "It's you! You've painted yourself as the beheaded monster! Why would you do that?"

Caravaggio grinned. "Too cheap to hire a model."

"That can't really be the reason," I said, wondering.

"Why not me? I'd like to think that I have the power to turn my enemies to stone. Now why don't you bring it to Del Monte and tell him I suggested he hire you."

"Me?" It seemed like too big an honor for a no-name servant.

Caravaggio grinned, turning from great artist into a young man with a twist of his lips. "He's in the alchemy chamber. Giovanni will show you."

I picked up the shield carefully. It was heavy and, like a real shield, had a strap in the back for an arm to go through. "Thank you," I murmured. "You're too kind."

Caravaggio hung up his cloak and picked up his palette, back to being a painter. We were dismissed; that was clear.

Giovanni led me down a narrow hall I hadn't noticed before. I'd thought we were on the top floor, but stairs led to an even higher level where the ceiling was lower, the rooms certainly smaller. Surely the master of the house wouldn't have a study in the attic?

"This is where the monsignor does his alchemy experiments and observes the heavens," Giovanni explained, rapping lightly on the first door we came to.

"Enter!" a low, honeyed voice called out.

Giovanni opened the door and led me inside. The narrow room was taken up with a long bench crammed with beakers of fluids, weights, a scale, dried herbs, heavy leather-bound books, a magnifying lens, even a telescope. Light streamed in through high windows and a hole in the ceiling.

The man hunched over the table was old, his round face creased with wrinkles, his beard white. Even so, there was a forceful dignity about him. He was used to giving orders, to being obeyed, but he looked up with kind, intelligent eyes and a patient smile.

"Yes?"

"Sir, my name is Marco, and I've been instructed by Maestro Caravaggio to present this painting he made for you and to ask you to allow me to work for you. I can read and write, and I'll do anything you ask." I spoke quickly, afraid I'd be kicked out the door before I could sell him on my skills. I held out the painting, hoping its clear magnificence would give me some value just because I'd delivered it.

"What a marvel!" Del Monte exclaimed, rising to take the painting from me. "Ferdinand will love this!" A few silent minutes passed as his eyes devoured the picture. "Himself," he said finally, turning to look at me. "He's painted himself as Medusa. Extraordinary."

I nodded. "He said that he would like to have Medusa's power."

Del Monte laughed, a deep, warm laugh. "I'm sure he would! But heaven help the pompous painters who crossed his path if he did!" He set the painting down gingerly on the table. "Tell me about yourself, Marco. Why should I hire you? Because Michele wants it so?"

"Michele?"

"Michele, Michelangelo. Our friend, the artist, Michelangelo Merisi da Caravaggio."

"Ah, of course," I stammered. "Yes, because he wants it, but also because I can read and write."

"So you said," Del Monte responded dryly. "And it's true that literacy is a rare gem, but surely you have other skills as well. Do you have scientific training, for example?"

I thought that being from the future would give me a technical advantage, but here I was, racking my brain for what could possibly be useful from eighth-grade science that would fit into sixteenth-century knowledge. "I've taken classes, signore," I said. "I know how to use a microscope, how to conduct experiments, how to write down data."

Now I really had Del Monte's attention. "Microscope? You've used a microscope?"

I desperately hoped the device had been invented as I nodded.

"I've heard of it from my friend Galileo Galilei. He calls it the little eye since it makes visible the very small. He promised to give me one. For now, I have his telescope. It's a different kind of lens. Instead of tiny things made larger, it makes things that are far away seem closer." Del Monte handed me an elegant leather and brass instrument, and gestured to the hole in the ceiling I'd noticed before. "This is how I observe the stars and the planets."

"I could help you with your records," I suggested. "Your observations of the phases of the moon, how Mars and Venus move through the sky. I've done that kind of thing in class before."

"You have?" Del Monte was stupefied. "Do you also have fine handwriting? Where did you say you studied?"

I wondered what university would sound the most impressive but also be too far away to check the truth of what I was saying. It would be easiest if I could speak English. I had it—Oxford! That had to be one of the oldest schools in the world and it happened to be in England.

"Oxford," I said, and continued in English more confidently. "I had some excellent teachers." I wasn't so sure about my handwriting, but my English was solid.

"For one so young, you're very learned! English, too. That is English, isn't it? I can manage French myself, but not English."

"Am I hired then, signore?" I didn't dare look him in the face but stared meekly at the ground.

"If your handwriting is clear enough, I'd like you to copy a book my friend Bruno sent me. It's an ancient Latin manuscript, very interesting, *On the Nature of Things* by Lucretius. For now, though, I need the room to myself. Come back after the afternoon meal and you can start copying."

I gave a clumsy bow, trying to look like an experienced servant and failing miserably. "As you wish, Your Eminence," I mumbled. Copying a book by hand? That sounded like a huge amount of work! And was my handwriting good enough? I could print okay, but if Del Monte wanted beautiful cursive, he was out of luck. I spent most of fourth grade complaining about the stupidity of learning handwriting when everything ended up typed anyway. Why hadn't I paid more attention then?

Giovanni had been silent the whole time but as we clattered down the stairs, he exploded. "You can read and write! You know English! You know science! Why did you come here as a kitchen boy?"

"I didn't know what else to do." That much was true.

"You're a sly one, Marco. What other secrets are you hiding?"

I laughed awkwardly. If he only knew!

The next couple of days I spent hunched over a table copying the book in Latin that Del Monte wanted. The pen was the kind made of a bird's feather that had to be dipped in ink. Which meant it was easy to mess up with blots and drips. Writing was tedious and slow, reminding me why I hated cursive in school. I had to pay extra attention since I didn't understand the words so it was easy to make mistakes with spelling as well as smudges. After only an hour, my fingers would be ink stained, my back aching, and my neck cramped. Why couldn't there be copy machines in the sixteenth century?

I was ready to give up, thinking I wasn't helping Mom this way anyway, when Del Monte offered me an Italian manuscript to work on instead.

"I need a copy of this sooner than the Lucretius, so could you do this one first?" He handed me a book called *The Expulsion of the Triumphant Beast* by Giordano Bruno. "You might have seen it when you were at Oxford. It was written while Bruno was in England."

I blushed as if I'd been caught in my lie. "No, somehow I missed this. I'd remember such a strange title."

Del Monte smiled. "It will make more sense once you've read the book."

I hoped I'd understand it better than the Latin I'd been copying so at least it would be less tedious. The book wasn't a story so much as different dialogues between two people. The one I liked best was a conversation about Zeus and his incredible attention to the details in everyday life. It was like a *Mad* magazine satire of a priest's sermon on how God sees everything and makes everything happen. Bruno asks the question, "Everything? Every little, teeny, tiny, unimportant thing?"

Here's an example of one passage:

"Zeus has ordained that today at noon two melons in Franzino's melon patch will be perfectly ripe, but that they will not be picked for another three days, by which time they will be judged no longer good enough to eat. He wishes that, also at noon, thirty jujubes, perfectly ripe, be picked from the jujube tree standing at the base of Mount Cicala on Giordano Bruno's property; thirty of them should be picked perfectly ripe, seventeen should fall to the ground unripe, and fifteen should be worm-eaten.

"Zeus ordained that Vasta, Albenzio's wife, while curling her hair, shall burn fifty-seven of them close to her forehead because she overheated the iron, but that she will not burn her head, that she will not swear this time when she smells the stench but instead be patient about it all.

"He ordained that from the dung of Vasta's ox, two hundred fifty-two dung beetles will be born, of which fourteen will be stepped on by Albenzio's foot and die, twenty will die by flipping over on their backs, twenty-two will live in the cellar, eighty go on pilgrimage through the courtyard, forty-two go live under that block of wood by the door, sixteen will roll their balls of dung wherever they like and the rest run about as they want."

I couldn't help laughing as I copied this, picturing the dung beetles scurrying around and Albenzio's foot being the Heel of Doom for them.

It was a strange manuscript for a powerful cardinal to have, mocking people who took religion so literally, but something about it made me think it could be important to Mom. Maybe my job was to do exactly this: make more copies of this book poking fun at strict religious ideas. Last time I went into the past, Mom had told me to look out for intolerance, for injustice. This strange book seemed like a cure for narrow-mindedness. That had to mean something. And if nothing else, my handwriting was finally getting much better.

When I'd finished enough pages for the day, Giovanni showed me around Rome, as he'd promised. I thought I was used to the way people dressed—in tunics and leggings or blouses and tight pants, elegant feathered hats or shapeless leather bonnets—until we came to a neighborhood where the men all had beards and wore strange yellow hats.

"Are they part of a club or something?" I asked Giovanni. "Why the same kind of hat?"

Giovanni stared at me as if I'd wondered why the sky was blue. "Haven't you seen a Jew before?"

My stomach pitched, and I suddenly felt like I was about to lose my breakfast. "What do you mean?" I quavered.

Giovanni shrugged. "Jews. They're Jews. They always dress like that."

"But why?" I felt like a bright yellow hat was about to sprout on my head, labeling me a Jew, too.

"It's the law, of course." Giovanni seemed annoyed. "Good Christians need to know if someone's a Jew, so it's easiest having them marked like that. It's been that way for centuries."

Now I really felt sick. If Giovanni knew I was Jewish, he wouldn't want to be near me. How could I be friends with someone I wasn't honest with? And what kind of Jew was I if I hid who I really was?

"We're in the ghetto. That's why there are so many of them," Giovanni explained as if he were describing a rat infestation.

"Perhaps the gentleman would like some fine velvet? A good silk? We have the best quality," a man wheedled while shoving a bolt of deep red cloth shot through with silver embroidery under Giovanni's nose.

"Be off!" Giovanni recoiled, grimacing in disgust. "These Jews—they're so pushy!"

I watched the cloth seller slink off, ashamed of him. Ashamed of the salesman, not Giovanni. I didn't want to be that kind of Jew. And just because we were both Jewish didn't mean I had to like or defend him. But I couldn't shake the sour feeling in my stomach, the corrosive shame roiling inside me.

"Diamonds, sir, of the highest purity. This way, sir." Another man sidled up to Giovanni, this one shorter and wider than the first, with rubbery jowls covered by a sparse beard. "Your master will be entranced by them!"

"Away, all of you!" Giovanni roared, furious now. "I shouldn't have taken the shortcut through the ghetto. Too many vermin here!"

The jeweler ducked quickly into his store.

Giovanni guided me through a narrow passage, careful to give all the yellow-hatted people a wide berth. I couldn't understand the mix of anger and shame surging through me. I was proud to be Jewish, and I should have defended the peddlers to Giovanni—they were just plying their trade, after all. But I didn't feel any kinship with these strange Jews with their odd hats and suspicious stares. The only connection I felt was to Giovanni. How could I be angry at him?

"That's a baptistery." He pointed to a small domed building jutting out from the wall. "It was put here to convert the Jews, but they're a stubborn people so it hasn't been very successful."

Now, now I should say something, but I couldn't.

"Good thing, too, I suppose," Giovanni added as we left the high walls of the ghetto behind. Here the streets were full of the usual crowds, not a yellow hat to be seen. "They lock the gates at night to keep the Jews in, but my master says they're a useful people. If you need a potion to cure you, they have the best physicians."

Some stereotypes are thousands of years old, I guess. As long as he hadn't noticed how clammy and sweaty I'd become, we could still be friends. I wanted to forgive Giovanni his prejudices, telling myself he was just repeating what he'd been told. But I wasn't sure I could forgive myself. I hadn't stood up for my own people. I hadn't even liked them.

By the time we came to the Forum, I wasn't angry at Giovanni or even hurt by him, but I was still furious with myself. I was supposed to be on guard for injustice, but what if I was the one being unfair? Was I unfair or just cowardly? Or were the two things the same? I didn't know what to think, what was right, but I couldn't erase the sickening shame that gripped me.

Only when the images of the ghetto were replaced by ancient columns and magnificent arches choked with weeds did I allow myself to relax a little. Marble pillars reached into the blue sky, holding up imaginary roofs. Others lay felled on the ground like trees. Cows, goats, sheep all grazed around what had been ancient Roman buildings.

"Don't people care about these ruins?" I asked, relieved to talk about something other than Jews. "They're totally neglected."

"Care about?" Giovanni looked at me as if I was a puzzle to solve. "The wealthy use this rubble for building material, and artists sometimes sketch the reliefs on the arches. What else do you expect people to do with any of this?"

"Don't you care about the history of your own city? This is history!" I could hear Malcolm yelling the words into my ear. He would be furious if he knew how Romans had treated their own cultural treasures. And even angrier if he knew how they treated Jews. Shame jolted through me again. Malcolm would have defended those peddlers. He would have done the right thing.

Giovanni seemed to think the Forum was like a giant wrecking yard for cars, junk for the most part, though somebody could pull out useful parts if they really dug around. I couldn't yell about the ghetto, but I could about the Forum.

"You said it yourself—these are ruins." Giovanni said, perplexed. "Meaning 'not useful, destroyed.' If they were complete, they'd be used. I'll show you."

We wove our way around cows and cow plops, columns broken off like tree stumps, and columns still standing and holding up elaborate capitals to the chill-whitened sky. We

passed by an arch that seemed complete, untouched by time amid all the wreckage.

I was surprised to recognize a menorah carved as part of the sculpted relief. Strange to come from the ghetto and find this. I couldn't help thinking that Mom had planned on this, that she was giving me some great lesson in my heritage. Was I supposed to do something for the Jews here? Was I supposed to protect them whether I liked them or not?

Of course, I should! It's easy to defend people you like. The hard thing is supporting those you don't. It was okay that I didn't feel a connection to the ghetto Jews the way I did to Giovanni, so long as I stood up for them. I promised myself I would, the next chance I got.

I studied the relief, trying to read its meaning. Was it the original story of Hanukkah, of the Maccabees rededicating the Temple after it was destroyed by Antiochus? I tried to dredge up the details from Hebrew school, but mostly I remembered the dreidel game and the miracle of the oil.

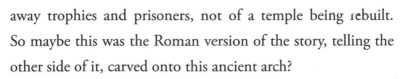

I wasn't sure who the Maccabees were fighting when the great miracle of Hanukkah happened, but I thought it was a Syrian-Egyptian king, not a Roman. And the story told in stone was one of soldiers ripping away trophies and prisoners, not of a temple being rebuilt. So maybe this was the Roman version of the story, telling the other side of it, carved onto this ancient arch?

I doubted Giovanni would know since these bits and pieces were like a giant junkyard to him, but I asked anyway. "Do you know the story behind this arch? Why are the men carrying a menorah?"

Giovanni gaped, as if he'd never really looked at the arch before. "I don't know what a menorah is, and I don't know the story, but Caravaggio could tell you. He has some friends who study old monuments like this, though I'm not sure why." Giovanni shrugged. The subject clearly didn't interest him.

He kept on walking, but I couldn't tear myself away from the arch. The menorah seemed like a secret message just for me. Was it a clue to the injustice I had to fix? Was I somehow supposed to find this menorah and have it returned to the Jews of Rome? And then I saw it: a corner of paper folded and tucked into a chip of the base. I pulled it out and stuck it in my pocket, trotting to catch up with Giovanni. I didn't have to read it to know it was from Mom.

"See!" Giovanni opened his arms wide, showing me the Colosseum, the same building that was on Mom's postcard. I grinned. No wonder she had chosen the arch as a mailbox! It had nothing to do with the menorah; she must have known I'd track down her postcard.

How many times had I seen the Colosseum in movies? It's one of those places everyone knows, like the Eiffel Tower, the Statue of Liberty, or the Great Wall of China. But seeing it in person was different. It was bigger than I'd imagined, towering and powerful. It felt old, like you could see time in the stones themselves.

And it was beautiful, despite the wooden joists buttressing the walls, the part that had fallen in on itself, and the stray stones littering the ground around it. What was left was strangely elegant, from the proportions of the arches to the fine chiseling of the numbers carved over each arch, kind of like a modern stadium numbering system. And maybe it had been used the same way, who knew?

"Monks live here now," Giovanni said. "It was a wool factory for a while, a place where women who used to be prostitutes could earn a living, but that didn't work out, so now it's a monastery."

"People live in the Colosseum?"

"Yes. That's useful, isn't it?" Giovanni grinned. It seemed more like sacrilege to me, but he looked so proud that he could show me a ruin that wasn't ruined, I didn't have the heart to disagree.

"Lucky monks," I said instead. "To live in such a historic place."

"I don't know how fortunate they are. I'm sure the roof leaks and the nearest fountain for water isn't close by, but monks aren't supposed to care about comfort."

"Can we go in?" I didn't care about the monks. I just wanted to see the famous arena where gladiators fought, where Christians were thrown to the lions, where the emperor gave a thumbs-up or thumbs-down to seal a fighter's fate.

Giovanni shook his head. "No point. There's nothing in there but monks and a pile of rubble. I can show you much more interesting things. You still haven't seen St. Peter's, and that's the biggest splendor in all the city!"

I almost insisted but decided it would be better to go back on my own. For now, I wanted to do the things that mattered to Giovanni.

I couldn't help finding myself drawn to Giovanni. As we walked back through the Forum and up the Capitoline Hill, I imagined what it would be like to touch his soft cheek, to feel his lips on mine. And with a jolt, I realized who he reminded me of—the other boy I'd felt this way about, the one I'd met in nineteenth-century Paris, Claude. They didn't look alike, but there was something in the eyes, in the way they smiled, in the tilt of their heads, the gesture of their hands. They carried themselves alike. And their voices, one in Italian, one in French, could be twins.

"You wanted to see the wonders of Rome, right?" Giovanni asked. "This is one of them!"

I stared at Giovanni, seeing the ghost of Claude hover over his face.

"Marco, are you all right?"

"Of course!" I blinked, trying to erase the double image, to see only Giovanni. But now that I'd made the connection, I couldn't forget it. I didn't know what to make of the coincidence. What did it mean? I thought I'd never see Claude again, but a wisp of him was here by me now in Giovanni.

"Marco?"

"I'm fine," I said, grinning. As I turned to see where my friend was pointing, a strange happiness bubbled up inside me. Two palazzos faced each other on the crest of the hill overlooking the Forum. They were like mirror images of each other with the same perfect geometrical balance and proportion. Like Giovanni and Claude, I thought, echoes of each other. In between them stood an impressive bronze statue of a man on a horse.

"The sculpture is ancient, some old Roman emperor, but the facades of the two palazzos, the geometric pattern on the floor of the piazza, the placement of the bronze in the middle, even the broad steps going down toward the Palazzo Venezia, they were all designed by Michelangelo."

"You mean, Michelangelo de Caravaggio? I thought he was a painter."

"No, I mean the other Michelangelo—Buonarroti, the Florentine. He was a painter, sculptor, and architect."

"The one who painted the Sistine Chapel?" As I said it, I wondered if I'd get to see it. But I wasn't in the past to sightsee. I had a job to do, if I could figure out what that was, whether it had to do with the Jews in the ghetto, the menorah on the arch, or Del Monte. I fingered the note in my pocket. The answer was probably in it.

I'd thought I should wait until I was alone before opening it, but I remembered that Giovanni couldn't read. I didn't have to worry about him looking over my shoulder. It was strange to think that something I took for granted—that everybody could read—wasn't true. I'd always thought there was something magical about reading and writing, but here, now, it truly was magical.

"What do you think?" Giovanni interrupted my thoughts.

"It's beautiful," I said, admiring the classical march of arches across Michelangelo's building, the weaving of lines into a radiating star on the ground, the gentle slope of broad steps down into the city. "I didn't think you could design a piazza, that it was just empty space."

Giovanni took my hand and hustled me down the stairs. "And now I'll show you another of his great designs."

Any thought of the note flew out of my head as soon as Giovanni's hand touched mine. I worried he could tell how hard my heart was racing. But his face was serene, excited by Michelangelo, not by me. And by the time we were at the bottom of the steps, he'd dropped my hand as naturally as he'd picked it up.

I swallowed my disappointment and gripped the note again. I had to stop letting Giovanni distract me. The street was broader here, less crowded than the narrow alleys near Del Monte's, so I could risk reading while walking and not get run over by a cart or bump into a peddler.

I opened the note and quickly scanned it. There were only two words, in Mom's handwriting, so it was easy:

Giordano Bruno

I crumpled up the note and quickly veered around a suspicious, foul-smelling mound. So nothing about the ghetto. I wouldn't have to stand up for the Jews as I'd promised myself, which was both a relief and a letdown.

Giordano Bruno. The name was familiar. And then I remembered! He was the friend who had given Del Monte the book by Lucretius. He was the author of the strange manuscript I was copying. I'd had a hunch it mattered to Mom. Who was he, and why was his book important enough to be duplicated?

I tried to remember everything I'd copied so far, searching for some clue in its meaning. I'd thought it was clever and funny. But there were serious parts, too, where he talked about how everything was made up of the same essential matter. According to him, Zeus and all creation consisted of tiny particles. He even called them atoms, the same way we do today.

I hadn't thought people knew about atoms until much later, so maybe that was the important part.

If only I could figure it all out!

We continued past grand homes of the rich, churches, and rickety wooden buildings, all on the same street. Lacquered coaches pulled by fine horses squeezed next to heavy drays, which clomped next to donkey carts. Where were we going?

We came to a narrow river and a marble bridge crossing it.

"The Tiber," Giovanni explained. "And on the other side of it, you can see the dome of St. Peter's."

To the right, a circular fortress loomed, topped by an enormous marble angel spreading its wings over the red stone building. To the left, a broad church was being built. The finished dome floated above the construction, designed, Giovanni told me, by Michelangelo. Looking at it, I forgot all about Bruno.

"No one could figure out how to span the immense space of the church until Buonarotti submitted his plans. Come inside and you'll see more proof of his genius."

Giovanni steered me past the workers on scaffolding and through the tall, thick doors into a space so vast that it felt otherworldly. The columns were as big as redwood trees, and the vault soared over our heads much higher than I remembered in Notre Dame in Paris. Panels of marble sectioned off the walls and floors, like in the Pantheon, but because of the scale, the sensation was one of great power, not of serenity.

"It's beautiful," I whispered, hushed by the immensity.

"Here is something even more beautiful." Giovanni pointed to a side chapel where a marble sculpture of the Virgin Mary cradling her dead son in her lap gave off a celestial glow.

I'd seen photos—this was Michelangelo's famous *Pietà*.

I fingered the sketchbook in my pocket. I'd been drawing as much as I could since I got here, hoping that being around so much great art would rub off on me and make me a better artist, but now, in front of such genius, I felt ashamed of my scrawls. No matter how much I drew, I'd never come anywhere close to this. I was just playing at art, not a real artist at all.

"Do you know the story?" Giovanni asked. I shook my head. I couldn't take my eyes off the graceful tilt of Mary's head, heavy with grief.

The marble seemed to have different textures for Jesus' curly beard, Mary's heavy drapery, and her slim fingers pressing into her son's flesh. How did he do that, I wondered, make stone breathe as if it were alive?

"When Michelangelo first made this, there was a lot of criticism that he made the Virgin so young, like a maiden. And here was Christ looking older than his mother. Michelangelo argued that Mary's purity kept her young. She wasn't plagued with the sins that age normal women. But he was so angered by the stupid comments that he hung around, waiting to hear what people would say when they saw his work.

"He was listening when a man boasted that another artist had made the masterpiece. That night, Michelangelo snuck back into St. Peter's and carved his name across the ribbon on Mary's chest. Do you see it? It's the only work he ever signed."

Latin letters on the broad sash read: MICHAELAGELUS BONAROTUS FLORENTIN FACIEBA.

"Michelangelo Buonarotti, the Florentine, made this?" I guessed.

Giovanni nodded. "Not that I know Latin, but that's what people say."

The letters reminded me of the ones I'd seen on the outside of the Pantheon. They had the same imperial Roman weight. I smiled, thinking that they were the answer a genius gave to his critics. First people said he should have carved Mary differently. Then they said someone else entirely had made the sculpture. Which kind of criticism was worse?

The Latin words had a soft glow, a halo of light around them. I felt them pull at me, an urgent tug, and without thinking, I stretched out my hand and gently touched the artist's name.

The floor tipped under my feet, and the marble columns swirled away in a dusky dance. Giovanni vanished in a cloud of purple haze. I felt dizzy as the stars and moon whirled around me. The *Pietà* was a touchstone.

When the ground settled and my head stopped spinning, I found myself back in another work of Michelangelo's, the church near the train station. The brass meridian stretched along the floor, the zodiac signs pacing on either side of it. Tourists in jeans with cameras strolled along the nave. And there in a side chapel were Dad and Malcolm.

"You waited for me!" I gasped, running up to them.

"Waited?" Dad asked. "What for?"

"Didn't you notice I was gone?" I wiped the sweat from my face, trying to calm my racing heart.

"Did you just time-travel?" Malcolm squinted at me, as if searching for some sign of temporal dust.

"Yes! I was in the sixteenth century! Rome was so different then. And the same." I shook my head. It was hard to explain.

"I met a painter, Caravaggio. And another man, Cardinal Del Monte, who knows Galileo." I was so excited that I couldn't help babbling. "I thought maybe that was why I was there, to save Galileo. Then I thought I should help the Jews—they're herded into a walled-in ghetto and have to wear these weird yellow hats."

"That's terrible!" Malcolm frowned. "Like the yellow stars that Hitler forced on the Jews?"

"Yes! Exactly! Except the Jews weren't being killed. They were just kept apart."

"You have to do something! Maybe those hats are a clue that if you can stop the Jews from wearing them, the Holocaust won't happen." Malcolm looked so outraged that he would have hurled himself into the past if he could have.

"Calm down," Dad said. "That sounds like wishful thinking, Malcolm. Mom said she's changing your future, not that of all Jews."

"But if you could change that, don't you have a moral duty to do so? Forget about us!"

The familiar curdling of shame filled my stomach. Why couldn't I be like that? Why did I let Giovanni say those terrible things about the Jews in the ghetto? I couldn't look Malcolm in the eyes.

Dad sighed. "That's not how it works. At least as far as I understand it. Mom said some events were so huge that they're impossible to change."

"What's the point, then?" Malcolm asked in disgust. "When you can't affect the things that really matter?"

There was no good answer for that. Instead Dad turned to me. "Do you know what you're supposed to change? Did you see Mom? Get a message from her?"

"I didn't see her, but she left me a note with a name on it, Giordano Bruno. So as much as I may want to help the Jews, that's not my job. I have to save Bruno."

"Who's Bruno? Maybe he's Jewish!"

"I doubt that. Would a cardinal have a Jewish friend? Read books written by a Jew? It doesn't seem likely." As much as I wanted to encourage Malcolm, I couldn't.

"So you've met this guy?" My brother sounded disappointed.

I explained about my job copying books and told everything I could remember about Bruno's work.

"We need to do some research, help you figure this out. Maybe Bruno is part of a secret cabalistic cult. He might have a Jewish connection you don't know about."

Dad nodded. "But first let's dump our luggage at the hotel and wash up a bit."

"Good idea." Malcolm sniffed me. "You smell funny. Is that what the sixteenth century smells like?"

"That's rich, coming from someone whose socks are a hazardous waste zone!" I shot back.

"Can I see the note?" Dad scanned it quickly. "Nothing

about Jews. Not a word about Galileo, just this Bruno fellow. We need to figure out who he was."

"Everyone knows that the Inquisition spared Galileo's life," Malcolm added. "He doesn't need your help."

"But maybe that happened because of something Mom and I did in the past. If I don't go back and do it now, then there will be a different ending. He could be executed."

Malcolm shook his head. "Whoa! That's circular logic! You're saying you have to save Galileo because you already *have* saved him?"

"Exactly! At least I think so. Or I thought so until I found Mom's note."

"Any other clues?" Dad asked.

"Is her rancid odor a clue?" Malcolm couldn't let it drop. Probably the only time in my life I stank more than he did, and he'd never let me forget it.

I glared at Malcolm but didn't take the bait. "I met Mom's old time-traveler friend, Morton. He took me to Del Monte's palazzo. According to him, Mom wanted me to work there while she worked in the Pope's household. Doesn't that sound like she's worried about the Inquisition? Which could mean this is a Jewish problem after all."

"Maybe." Dad looked thoughtful.

"Let's start now by learning about this Bruno guy," Malcolm said. "I could go to an Internet café while you leave our stuff at the hotel."

"Let's stick together," Dad said. "We have time for research."

"Except we never know when Mira will disappear on us. We have to help her be better prepared next time!" Malcolm's eyes flashed with determination. I wanted to give him a big hug. All his stinky comments were totally forgiven.

"Mira, promise not to touch anything!" Dad ordered.

"I won't! I'll try not to, really." I hoped this was a promise I could keep.

It was strange to walk on the same old streets. They looked both entirely different and strangely similar to where I'd walked centuries earlier. There were cars now and wide boulevards where there'd been only narrow lanes, but many of the buildings looked the same. They were the same actually, a strange blend of ancient ruins embedded in medieval walls or Renaissance architecture, as if you could see the layers of time, bits added onto bits in a mix of centuries and styles.

The streets were chaotic with scooters weaving around cars and buses, tourists following guides holding up brightly colored flags, monks, nuns, and regular people, Romans and tour groups.

We dumped our bags in our tiny hotel room, and I took a long shower, washing off ancient kitchen grease and who knows what else. It felt like an incredible luxury. While I scrubbed, Malcolm used the computer in the hotel lobby.

"Here's what I learned," he announced after I had changed

into fresh clothes and we were ready to go out. "The Jews of Rome were actually treated pretty decently for the time. The Inquisition didn't bother them, and they could run businesses and make money as long as they lived in the ghetto. They were forced to go to Mass once a week, but that's minor compared to the way other cities treated the Jews."

"Malcolm, this isn't about the Jews! The fact that the Inquisition left them alone is proof of that." I didn't want to describe how the men in the ghetto didn't feel like distant relatives or family. They were totally weird strangers, people I didn't feel at all connected to.

"Here's another interesting factoid," Malcolm continued obliviously. "Did you know the word 'ghetto' comes from Italian? From 'borghetto' or 'little borgo.' 'Borgo' means neighborhood, and the first ghetto was in Venice. You can still see the walls and the gate that was locked every night."

"What about Bruno?" I pushed down the shame curdling in the pit of my stomach, reminding me that I hadn't stood up for my own people, something my brother definitely would have done.

"He wasn't Jewish. In fact, he was a monk, but mostly he was a scholar. He taught at universities all over Europe and wrote a lot of books. He did read Jewish mystical writings, like the Kabbalah, so there might be a connection there."

"Malcolm, I keep telling you, forget the Jews." I didn't want there to be a connection—there couldn't be one! "It's about Bruno. Mom said so. What else did you discover?"

"That's all I had time for."

"That's a good start," Dad said. "Let's see something of the city, and then we can do more research."

"Good idea," I agreed. I wanted to see what had changed, how much of ancient Rome remained. We'd have plenty of time for research after that.

Dad wanted to see St. Peter's first and thought our hotel was too far to walk, that we should take a cab. I insisted that we could easily go on foot and we'd see more of the city. Malcolm agreed, not that he had any sense of the distance, but he wanted to walk, no matter how far it was.

"That's the best way to see a new city anyway, to wander around and get lost."

"We're not getting lost," I said. How much could the streets have changed? I led the way, passing familiar buildings and baroque fountains that were new to my sixteenth-century sense of the city. The big circular castle topped with the marble angel on the other side of the river, the Castel Sant'Angelo, was exactly the way I remembered it, but now the bridge in front of it was lined with

angel statues. St. Peter's was finished, with not only a facade but two arching colonnades framing the piazza in front of it, like arms embracing the tourists.

Only before, we had walked right in, passing beggars, peddlers, donkeys pulling carts, but now a line snaked along one side of the church.

"Don't tell me we have to pay to go into a church? How tacky can you get?" I said, exasperated.

"We don't have to pay." Dad smiled. "That's in Florence where they charge you to enter any church. But we have to go through a security screening."

"You're kidding!" Malcolm rolled his eyes. "What's the Pope afraid of? Doesn't he have God on his side?"

"It's not a joke," Dad said. "Somebody tried to kill Pope John Paul II not too long ago, and some maniac took a hammer to Michelangelo's statue inside, trying to smash the *Pietà*."

"What?" I gasped, my stomach lurching. "It's so beautiful, so perfect! How could anyone want to destroy it? Did they ruin it?"

"You're not worried about the Pope, just the statue," Malcolm teased. "Way to show some compassion, Mira."

"Well, the Pope survived his attack—Dad said someone *tried*. But what about the *Pietà*?"

"Don't worry," Dad said, as the line slowly snaked forward. "It's fine. Mary's nose was broken, but it's been restored."

The line moved pretty quickly and soon we were walking up the steps to the central doors. Signs advised us that no bare shoulders or shorts were allowed, another odd modern touch—you didn't need that kind of finger-shaking in the sixteenth century.

But stepping inside, I had the same sense of vastness, of being held in a place suspended between heaven and earth. Even the light slanting onto the marble floor seemed more sacred somehow. I went right to the side chapel with the *Pietà*. And there it was, only now it was behind a thick sheet of glass. No way I'd get near enough to touch it. I didn't realize how lucky I'd been to see it so close. I could still admire it, but the force of its beauty was dimmed by the smudged glass and the crowds of tourists taking pictures with their camera phones.

Still, I couldn't resist repeating the story Giovanni had told me, how Michelangelo, great artist though he was, had been criticized, how this was the only thing he'd ever signed.

Malcolm nodded approvingly. "Not bad! This time-travel stuff is making you a historian. Or an art historian. You still draw, don't you?"

"Not really." I hadn't shown my brother my sketches for years now; they were too embarrassing. I'd drawn a lot since we'd been in Rome. There were so many amazing things I wanted to capture, but I didn't feel like I'd done a good job with any of them.

"This would be a great place for sketching. If I had your talent, I'd have a pen in my hand right now."

"You think I'm good?"

"Your problem is you've always been too critical of yourself. If something's not absolutely perfect, you think it's terrible."

"That's not true!" I said, though it kind of was.

"If you could draw what you saw in the past, that would be so amazing! It's as close as I can come to time-traveling with you. Come on, Mira, you've got to try!"

I could feel the tips of my ears turning pink. How could I admit I had been sketching all along? And even if I owned up to my lie, how could I let him see my sketchbook? The only person I'd shown was Claude, in nineteenth-century Paris. I blushed at the memory of that strangely intimate moment, my whole face burning as much as my ears.

"What is going on with you, Mira?" Malcolm peered at me intently. "I'd swear you're hiding something."

"No, I'm not," I mumbled, wishing I was a better liar.

"You are! I can see right through you!"

"Malcolm, leave your sister alone." Dad came to my

rescue. "I'm starving! Let's find a good trattoria and have a real Roman meal."

"I'm not letting you off the hook so easily!" Malcolm wagged a finger at me. "If you have pictures of the past you're hiding from me…"

"I don't—really! But maybe I'll draw something next time." I wasn't promising anything, but I had to say something to get Malcolm to drop the subject.

"Come on, guys," Dad urged. "Pizza! Pasta!"

We found a restaurant on a small street nearby where tables were set outside and the smells of the food being served were too appetizing to pass by. My stomach growled. All I'd eaten in the sixteenth century had been beans and bread. No pasta at all. When I'd asked Giovanni, he'd told me pasta was for special occasions and only for the wealthy. Not for the likes of me. Now that I could, I ordered a heaping plate of pasta alla carbonara. The bacony tomato sauce was rich and spicy and totally satisfying after so many days of boring beans.

I wanted to focus only on the meal, and luckily, Malcolm was so busy stuffing his face that he forgot to nag me about drawing anymore. Instead he and Dad got into a complicated argument about the Vatican Secret Archives and how they could possibly sneak in to find out about Bruno. It all sounded too James Bond or *Da Vinci Code*-ish to be useful in real life. And anyway, the carbonara was much more important.

After lunch Dad wanted me to show him where Del Monte lived. I wondered if I'd know how to get there, but after crossing the bridge with the angel statues, my feet found their way along a familiar curving street, past Piazza Navona, which now had three big fountains along the center of it.

On the other side of Piazza Navona, we came out onto the street facing Palazzo Madama, Del Monte's home, only now it had the Italian and European Union flags flying over the central door, and police officers and soldiers stood guard. I pointed to the building.

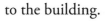

"That's it," I said. "But it looks like an official building now."

"It's the Italian Senate building," Dad said, looking through his guidebook. "Interesting. But no way we can go in."

"How about we see the church around the corner instead? It's Del Monte's favorite. He told me he wanted to be buried there."

Walking past the palazzo, I half expected to see Giovanni emerge from the side door, the one I'd gone in as a kitchen servant. But there were only more sentries in bright blue uniforms with gold braid on their shoulders and shiny black boots.

We meant to look for Del Monte's tomb, but a cluster of tourists, all crowded around a chapel on the left side of the nave, suggested there was something more interesting to see. And there was! Large labels proudly introduced three paintings by Caravaggio, two on each side of the chapel and one in the center. The central image made me gasp. A bald old man was writing down the gospel as it was dictated to him by an angel fluttering over his head. The angel was Giovanni.

Malcolm sputtered, pointing to the painting on the left. "See, the young man in the yellow shirt! He looks just like you! You posed for Caravaggio?"

"No." I shook my head. "I didn't." Though I had to admit the face looked suspiciously like mine. "Maybe he just remembered me?" Would Caravaggio think I was worth painting? That didn't seem likely. Maybe I had a really ordinary face. The figure wasn't my twin after all, just very similar.

Dad put his arm around me, grinning. "My daughter in a famous picture!"

"Dad, you're embarrassing me!" I leaned closer. Was that

really me? It was strange proof that I really had been in the six-teenth century, that a famous artist had cared what I looked like.

"Wow," said Malcolm. "This is the guy you met? Incredible." I felt bad for Malcolm. He could have been jealous and spiteful, but he was simply in awe. He was too nice a brother to be mean to me, too passionate an historian not to be interested.

Maybe Caravaggio had painted Mom, too. I studied the other painting for any clues. And there he was, in the face of the man farthest back, the one turning to look at Matthew reaching for the palm of martyrdom—it was Caravaggio! He was older than when I met him, with a mus-tache and close-cropped beard, but it was defi-nitely him.

I pointed him out, relieved to change the subject from my own strange appearance in the companion picture.

Then I described how the first painting I'd seen by Caravaggio had been one of his own chopped-off head as Medusa.

"You're kidding, right?" Malcolm asked. His eyebrows shot up like excited punctuation marks. "The guy must have had some serious issues!"

I shrugged. "Look at the ceiling, at those pale, dried-out figures. That's the way everyone else painted while Caravaggio was doing this kind of amazing stuff. He was brilliant, and aren't all geniuses kind of weird?"

"Maybe." Dad smiled. "We don't know the stories about the ones who lived long ago, but when you think about people like Picasso or Edison or Einstein, they sure fit the weirdness model." He looked at his watch, though the idea of time fixed like that was a joke to me now. "As wonderful as it is to see you in a famous chapel, let's go to one more site, this time something that might qualify as a wonder for my book, okay? Then we can find an Internet café to do more research on Bruno."

My head was swimming with images—St. Peter's, the Pantheon, the Colosseum. I settled on the Pantheon for Dad's wonder, since that was the closest, only a few streets away.

It was timeless, as magnificent as ever. The only difference I could see on the outside was that all the bronze that had been on the ceiling of the portico had been stripped away. Dad read in his guidebook that the Barberini pope had it melted down to make the bronze altar with the twisted pillars designed by Bernini for St. Peter's. "The Romans said that what the barbarians didn't pillage, the Barberini did."

But inside, it was as purely serene as ever. The marble was still there, although now there were ornate tombs for the first Italian kings. Still it was surprisingly the

same. I stood in the center, looking up through the hole in the dome, watching thin wisps of clouds overhead. It was like a heavenly eye, looking down on us.

"This could definitely be a wonder," Dad said, setting up his camera. He seemed as impressed as I was.

"What about the Colosseum? Or St. Peter's?" Malcolm suggested.

"We'll see the Colosseum tomorrow." Dad yawned. "Right now I need a nap. Or some strong Roman coffee."

"If you sleep now, you won't get used to the new time zone. That's what you're always telling us," I reminded him. "Plus we still need to find how I can help Bruno."

"Coffee, then."

We sat down at a café facing the Pantheon. Men dressed as gladiators posed with tourists. Women in Renaissance velvet urged pamphlets about musical performances on passersby. Funny how even in modern Rome, you were always reminded of the past—not just by the remnants of it in the buildings, but by people trying to re-create it.

Dad and Malcolm sipped perfect cappuccinos while I drank an Italian soda and admired the fountain in the piazza, an obelisk, the same fountain I'd seen with Giovanni. I liked how so much hadn't changed in Rome over the centuries.

"Can I have a coin to throw in the fountain?" I asked Dad.

"You're supposed to do that in the Trevi Fountain, not this one." But he handed me a small coin anyway.

I tossed the coin into the water, wondering where Mom was, wishing she was safe and that I'd see her soon. I held onto the marble basin, leaning over to see where the thin silver disk had landed. I gasped as water gushed up around me, every drop crystal clear. Then a thick velvety blackness cloaked the glittery sparks of water. The sky tipped and time eddied around me in dizzying swirls of the sun and moon.

February 8, 1600

When I could see again, the café was gone. I closed my hands into fists, angry at myself. I really had to be more careful about touching things if I wanted any kind of control over time travel! The gladiators asking to be paid to pose with them had vanished. There were no cars, no bicycles, just the rancid smell of sewage and rotting vegetables. I was still in front of the Pantheon but back in the sixteenth century.

Well, not quite the sixteenth century. When I asked a passing monk for the date, he told me the exact day—the eighth of February, 1600. From the cold, brisk air and the heavy gray rain clouds massing overhead, I already knew it was winter.

I shivered despite the heavy wool cloak I was wearing, the same clothes I wore the last time. Four years had passed since I'd seen Giovanni, Del Monte, and Caravaggio. Could I go back to the palazzo? Would anyone recognize me or let me in? What explanation could I give for my strange absence? I'd last seen Giovanni in St. Peter's. I worried that if he'd seen me disappear, he'd think I was a sorcerer. That could be dangerous in the time of the Inquisition.

But if he hadn't been looking right at me—and maybe he wasn't—I could come up with some kind of lame explanation. Maybe there were pirates in Rome, ready to kidnap unsuspecting fools into forced labor. Or maybe monks from the Inquisition had grabbed me by mistake.

I wanted to believe that Giovanni was a friend, that he'd believe whatever story I told him, but I realized I couldn't be sure of that. I thought of Claude, how he'd hated me for vanishing without a word. My stomach twisted at the idea that Giovanni might feel the same.

I clutched the cloak tightly to keep in its meager warmth and hurried through the streets to Palazzo Madama. All I knew was that I had to help Bruno, and that meant talking to Del Monte.

I knocked on the door that I'd last seen flanked by sentries in fancy, gold-braided uniforms. I didn't have to wait long before a thin, grubby boy answered. Probably the servant taking my place in the kitchen.

"I'm here to see Monsignore Del Monte," I said, trying to sound forceful, like I belonged there. It was easier to pretend to a boy than to hulking Carlo.

"At the servants' door?" the boy squeaked. "This is the tradesman entrance. The main door is around the corner, to your left."

"I know my way around!" I barked, imagining how Malcolm would act, hoping that the angrier I seemed, the less a servant would dare to question me. "I work for the cardinal. That's why I'm at this door. Just let me in!" I pushed my way past, praying that Carlo wasn't in the kitchen. I couldn't keep up this bravado in front of him.

Luckily, the familiar big room was empty, though the ingredients for a big feast were piled high on the central long table— pheasants, onions, potatoes, loaves of crusty bread, wheels of cheese, sprigs of herbs, braids of garlic.

The boy stared slack-jawed as I climbed the stairs, searching first for Giovanni, then for Caravaggio, but the room that last time had held those impressive paintings was now dusty and empty except for some trunks and baskets, clearly a place for storage, not an artist's studio. My heart sank. I didn't need to find Giovanni or Caravaggio, but I wanted to. Giovanni, with his shades of Claude, was the only friend I had in this strange time and place. If he was still my friend. A pretty big "if."

I knocked on the door to Del Monte's study and was relieved when his familiar deep voice called out, "Enter!"

Four years had aged the cardinal even more, drawing new

lines onto his face. He peered at me intently for a long moment while I waited to see if he would recognize me.

"Marco?" he said finally. "Is that you?" His eyebrows shot up to the top of his forehead in surprise.

"It is, Monsignore! You must forgive me my sudden disappearance."

"We thought you must have been killed, thrown into the river."

"Something like that." I decided to go with the kidnap story. "I was dragged from St. Peter's, knocked out, and found myself on a boat, conscripted into a crusade. It took me a while to find my way back." I was becoming a master of the on-the-spot lame excuse. "I know I didn't work for you very long last time, but I'm hoping to do a better job this time, if you'll have me."

"A crusade? Tell me something you learned during your adventure that will amaze me." Del Monte leaned forward eagerly.

What could I safely say? I didn't know anything about Bruno, but maybe I could use something Galileo had done. I remembered that he'd done some experiment where he dropped two things, one heavy, one light, from the Tower of Pisa, to see which would land first. And of course, he was famous for insisting that Copernicus was right—that the earth orbited the sun rather than the other way around.

"Well," I began, worried I was saying the absolute wrong thing to a cardinal. "There was a lot of talk about the theory that the earth moves around the sun. Some crusaders said that didn't change their belief in God, just changed the way they understood the seasons, the way the constellations change over the year."

"And you, what do you believe?" Del Monte leaned forward, staring so intently at me that I had to turn away. I couldn't hold his gaze.

"It's true," I mumbled, fear gripping my stomach. Was I committing heresy? Was it a crime to think this way?

"Amazing you should say that. It sounds like something written by my friend, Giordano Bruno." The cardinal's face lit up at the memory. "You know Bruno too! He wrote the Italian book you were copying when you worked here. Perhaps you found his theories interesting."

"I don't remember anything about the earth orbiting the sun," I admitted. "But I was impressed by what he said about everything being made of the same small particles mixed together in different combinations. Atoms, he called them."

"He didn't invent the term or the idea. That comes from Lucretius. Do you remember when you first came here?" Del Monte asked. "Before Bruno's book I asked you to copy a work in Latin. That book, by an ancient Roman philosopher, Lucretius, was the inspiration for many of Bruno's ideas. Like the notion you mention, that everything is made of tiny units of matter called atoms. That atoms collide and combine into the many different forms of things around us, including us. It's an idea the Church disagrees with."

The ancient Roman guy sounded very smart to me. He'd developed a theory about atoms long before there was any way to prove their existence. That made me think how much of science comes from our ability to imagine a possibility, to figure out how things could work, apart from any evidence. The idea has to come first. If the Church was telling people what they could and couldn't believe, how would anyone ever come up with scientific theories? How would anything new be invented?

"Why would the Church not like that?" I asked, though I had a sinking feeling I knew the answer.

Del Monte's face drooped with sadness. "The Church takes the Bible literally and if man was created in God's image, then we can't be made of the same material as a leaf or a dog. Lucretius and Bruno don't agree. And Bruno goes even further. Which is why he's been in prison now for many years, being examined by the Inquisition for heresy."

This sounded like exactly the kind of injustice Mom would want changed! Maybe I was supposed to convince Del Monte to help save his friend. Maybe I was supposed to somehow free Bruno from prison myself.

Del Monte went on to explain that Bruno wrote that there was more than one world, that this world existed alongside many others just like it but different as events took different paths. If the idea of atoms was basic physics, then this was much more complicated physics! I wondered if Bruno was talking about time travel. Did he think we could change what happened, or did he think there were parallel universes, each one different?

"I'd like to read that book if you have it," I said.

"Yes, of course, but you'd best read quickly. If Bruno is found guilty, the Inquisition is certain to put all his works on the list of banned books. The Church doesn't want people to be curious, to ask how things work." Del Monte sighed. "I thought that alone would make him recant—to risk not just his life, but his life's work like this..."

The cardinal shuffled over to a corner where books and papers teetered in piles. "Ah, that reminds me," he said, sorting through thick leather books and thin paper pamphlets, all covered in dust. "A letter came for you, years ago now, but I don't remember ever throwing it away. In fact, I'm sure I didn't. It must be here somewhere." He sifted through piles that looked like they hadn't been touched in far more than four years.

"Aha!" Del Monte triumphantly held up a small scroll tied with ribbon and sealed with wax.

"Who is it from?" I asked, though really it could only be from Mom or Morton.

"I don't recognize the seal," Del Monte said. "But I remember that it was brought by someone from the papal office, maybe someone from the Inquisition. You'll know once you open it, though by now whatever news it holds may not matter much."

I took the scroll, my fingers itching to open it right away. Instead I asked if there was any work I could do for the cardinal. Would he take me back on? Could I stay here, even if it meant sleeping in the kitchen? I had to be near him to get him to save Bruno.

"For a while, at least. I only needed a scribe to copy books that are illegal to print. But now it's easier to smuggle from Switzerland the works that the Church doesn't like." Del Monte's eyes lit up with a collector's passion. "Geneva and Basel are full of printers churning out books in a way I couldn't have imagined. My library keeps growing. But lately, all I can think about is how to soften Bruno's words so that he won't look so guilty."

"What else does Bruno believe?" I asked. "Did he do experiments like your friend, Galileo?" Funny that I'd never heard of Bruno before this trip when it sounded like he was being punished for the same thing Galileo was—or would be.

"Experiments? Observations, you mean." Del Monte picked up one of the books piled on the table in front of him. "Bruno is more of a philosopher than Galileo. Although he's written about mathematics." He opened the book to show me a drawing of geometric shapes. They seemed more like designs than math. But that was only one book of many. Del Monte described a book by Bruno about how to remember everything you ever read by using some kind of complicated system. (Who wants to remember everything like that, I wondered?) He wrote about physical matter and ideas, how everything and everyone were part of the divine.

"He sounds brilliant," I said. "Somebody to be honored, not condemned. You have so much influence. Surely you can help save him."

Del Monte shook his head. "I've talked with the Pope, with the chief Inquisitor, with the Spanish ambassador, with the Florentine ambassador, with everyone I can think of. The only person I haven't cajoled is Bruno himself, but only because I can't get into Tor di Nona prison to see him."

"Perhaps that's something I could do. I know I don't have wealth or rank or power, but wouldn't it be easier for a nobody like me to get into the prison?"

"Get into, yes. Get out of, I'm not so sure." Del Monte rubbed his forehead with his hands, as if trying to erase his worries. The gesture reminded me of Dad, and I felt a sudden pang of homesickness. "I appreciate the enthusiasm, Marco. And I'm happy to house you for a week or so while we figure out what exactly is happening. More than that, I can't promise."

"You're too kind, Monsignore!" I knew I shouldn't take up any more of the cardinal's time, but I had to ask. "And the painter, Caravaggio? He no longer lives here?"

Del Monte's face eased into a smile. "He's always welcome, but with what he earns for his pictures these days, he could buy his own palazzo. Not that he has. Instead, he rents rooms just up the street a bit. You'll see him at dinner one evening, I'm sure."

Which I hoped meant seeing Giovanni as well! I bowed and took my leave, feeling much better than when I'd entered the room. It didn't sound like Del Monte needed any urging to help Bruno. Maybe Mom knew that. I broke open the age-brittled seal and unfurled the scroll.

Dearest Mira,

    I've tried, but I can't do this by myself. I need your help. Save Bruno and then we can be together! I miss you all so much.

                               Love,

                               Mom

At least she didn't sound scared the way she had in the postcard. Now she sounded tired, desperate maybe. And I have to admit a teeny, tiny part of me was proud that she needed me, that I had to be here doing something to make a real difference.

And I was right. Bruno had to be saved. I could either try to see him or try to talk to someone in the Inquisition, make them soften so much he wouldn't need to recant. But if Del Monte couldn't convince them, would I be able to? It seemed worth a try, especially since I might find Mom at the Inquisition offices.

In the modern world, the Pope still has his own tiny country, Vatican City, circled by high walls next to St. Peter's. In the seventeenth century, before Italy became a unified country, the Papal States were a big chunk of territory around Rome. Still, I guessed the papal offices would be close to St. Peter's.

For a major city, Rome was easily crossed on foot. Walking from Del Monte's Palazzo Madama to St. Peter's didn't take long. To the right of the church, guards patrolled the entry to what in modern Rome was the back of the Vatican museum. What could I say to get past them? I wished I looked older, more commanding, or at least rich enough not to be questioned. It was one thing to push my way past a scrawny kid, another thing to face one of these sentries.

I was trying to come up with a plan when a scowling man in a plumed hat swept past the guards, straight toward me. At first I thought it could be Mom, angry that I'd come this close to her. Then I realized with a horrible shock that it was the beautiful woman from Paris, Madame L., the one Morton said was a Watcher. She was wearing men's clothes, but those piercing violet eyes, that jutting chin—it was definitely her. And she probably recognized me, in boy's dress myself!

I was too terrified to find out. I turned and ran, dodging past carts and peddlers, monks and beggars, women shouldering pails of water, and men carrying loaves of bread. When I thought I must be safe—and besides, I needed to catch my breath—I hunkered down beside a fountain, waiting for my heart to stop pounding.

A hand gripped my shoulder like an eagle's talon. "Waiting for me, are you?" Madame L. asked, yanking me to my feet. "I warned you not to trouble the past! I told you what would happen!" Flecks of spittle flew from her angry mouth. It was strange to see someone so gorgeous so furious. I tried to wrench away, but she was too strong.

"Let me go!"

Holding my arm tightly with one hand, she pulled my chin up with the other, drilling her eyes into mine as if she could see her way into my brain and all my guilty intentions. I stared back at her, suddenly angry myself. I should have been terrified, but all I felt was rage, enormous and black. Who was she to tell me what to do?

"Leave me alone!" I shouted, trying to stomp on her foot to shake her into releasing me.

"What is going on here?" A beefy man with a bloody apron

wrapped around his waist came out of the nearby butcher shop. "Should I send for the sbirri?"

"Not necessary," Madame L. said. "I can take care of this thief."

"I'm not a thief! This man's a liar! He's the thief!" I tried to look indignant, in control, but I felt panicky and trapped. The butcher clearly believed Madame, who was much more elegantly dressed than me. He grinned at me.

"Of course he is. He can steal my sausage once he's through with you." The butcher winked, wiping his dirty hands on his dirtier apron, and ducked back into his shop.

"Nobody can save you except yourself," Madame hissed into my ear. "Now give your mother this message—she has to stop now or she's risking your future as well as her own."

"You don't know me, and you don't know my future." I held myself up straight and tall. My rage gave me courage I didn't know I had.

"I'm warning you! If you break the laws of time travel, you *will* be punished." She leaned in closer, hissing into my face. "Your mother is lying to you. She's the one you should be mad at."

She reached for the fountain behind me. "I'll be watching you!" And with those words, she touched the stone edge of the fountain, vanishing in a blinding flash of yellow light. The air crackled with static electricity, but nobody else seemed to notice anything unusual. A man riding a donkey clopped by;

a woman carrying a basket of eggs hurried in the opposite direction. Time was flowing all around me, and I felt frozen, stuck where I stood. Was Madame L. right? Was Mom lying to me?

I wasn't sure where to go, what to do. Should I warn Mom about the Watcher? She must know. After all, Morton did. And she wouldn't want me coming close to her. I had to focus on Bruno, on my task here. But that was the problem. I didn't know *how* to help Bruno. If a powerful man like the cardinal was at a loss, what could I offer?

I walked the narrow streets, my nerves jangling, trying to calm down and think clearly. Rome, for all its big reputation, is a small city, so I found myself on the street where Del Monte said Caravaggio now rented rooms. I could be passing by his home and not even know it. I scanned windows and doors for any sign that a famous artist lived there.

That's when I saw Giovanni coming out of a candlemaker's shop. He hadn't changed much in four years. Maybe his shoulders were a little broader, but his hair was as golden as ever, his face as handsome. And when he recognized me, a familiar warm smile bloomed on his face. I blushed, remembering how I'd almost kissed Claude in nineteenth-century Paris.

"Giovanni!" I stammered, taking his hand in an awkward greeting. "I know it's been a while, but I feel I've known you for centuries. Do you remember me, Marco?"

"Of course! Where did you go? I didn't see you leave St. Peter's. You were just gone." He didn't seem angry that I'd vanished in front of him. More importantly, he didn't think I was a sinister wizard.

I told him the same lame story I'd told Del Monte, glossing over it quickly.

"I wondered what had happened," Giovanni said. "At first, I thought you were tricking me." He looked down at the memory, his cheeks turning pink. "I thought you were a robber, that you'd managed to pick my pocket. But I still had my money. Forgive me for thinking ill of you! It was only a passing suspicion."

"An understandable one!" I reassured him, smiling. Just being around him made me feel so much better. "What really matters is that I'm here now. I thought I'd find you at the cardinal's palazzo, but he told me Caravaggio had moved."

"Yes, he has his own rooms now. He's one of the most sought-after, highest-paid artists in the city." Giovanni looked proud, as if the accomplishment was his own. "Come with me and I'll show you the painting he's working on now."

I promised myself I wouldn't stay with him long. I would look for Mom, try to help Bruno, just not right now. We hadn't gone far when Giovanni knocked on the door of a rose-colored building with absolutely no indication that a famous artist worked inside. I'd never have found it by myself. It didn't look like Del Monte's elegant palazzo, and the woman who opened the door didn't look like the servant of a wealthy man. She had a weathered face and a skirt smudged with muddy red streaks. From killing a chicken possibly. Or a rabbit. She glared sullenly at Giovanni and let us in without a word of welcome.

"Who's that?" I whispered as Giovanni led me up the stairs to the top floor.

"That's the landlady," he answered matter-of-factly. "She and her daughter have the lower floors. We live above, where the light is best, the windows the biggest."

"If Caravaggio is so rich, why doesn't he have his own palazzo?" The rooms Giovanni showed me didn't look wealthy at all. There was barely any furniture in them, a smattering of books, some clothes hung on hooks. Most of the space was taken up by large canvases propped against the walls. One was on a low easel, all deep shadows and glowing light swatches with no definite shapes yet. It was interesting to see how Caravaggio worked, by casting light and loosely sketching the forms within it.

"Who needs a palazzo?" Caravaggio answered, startling me. I hadn't seen him, hidden as he was behind yet another canvas. "Then I'd need to hire servants, buy furniture, bother with stupid details like that. All I want is a place to paint, and the only servant I need is Giovanni."

Giovanni smiled proudly. "Signore, it's Marco. Remember him?"

"Marco? I don't remember a Marco, but any friend of

Giovanni is welcome here!" He emerged from the shadows and looked me up and down with a piercing gaze. For a moment I worried he could tell I was a girl, but really, how could he?

Giovanni hadn't aged much, but his master definitely had. Now he looked the way his self-portrait did in the painting Dad and Malcolm had admired in the church of San Luigi dei Francesi, with a beard and a mustache and wrinkles crinkling out from the corners of his eyes. Not a boy anymore, but a young man.

"You're just what I need," he pronounced, satisfied.

"For what?" I asked. "You said you didn't need any servants."

"But I do need models to pose for me. Here, try this on." He rummaged in a trunk behind him and handed me a yellow shirt and a plumed hat. I stared, gaping. This is what I was wearing in the other painting in the church! So I did pose for Caravaggio—I just hadn't by the time I saw the painting. But I had to have done so because the painting was there. I was so confused. Time seemed to slip between my fingers, changing shape constantly.

"Don't just stand there gawking," Caravaggio said. "It won't be hard. Just wear these things and sit by that table." He directed me into position, ignoring my protests while I quickly buttoned the yellow shirt over my tunic, trading my worn hat for his much more elegant one.

Giovanni laughed. "I've sat for the master many times, no harm done at all."

"But how do I stay still?"

"You'll manage," Caravaggio assured me, picking up the same palette made from a discarded painting that I remembered from before. He began to quickly move his brush over the canvas.

It was the oddest sensation. Time stood still while he painted. I didn't feel antsy or bored, but contained, riveted in place by his eyes, by the connection between me and his brush. I remembered watching Degas sketch his model with pastels when I was in nineteenth-century Paris. It had seemed so magical, seeing the marks emerge on the paper. This time I couldn't see what the artist was doing, but it was magic all the same. I was part of something bigger than myself.

But I was also leaving evidence that I'd been here, proof that I'd time-traveled. A shiver ran through me, chilling me. Would this be a crime to the Watcher? Was I changing the future just by being here, allowing myself to be painted? That seemed ridiculous, since Caravaggio could easily paint anybody else. Still, I worried about leaving my image behind. But I'd already done that. I'd seen the painting with Dad and Malcolm. So now I had no choice but to stay, right?

The whole way time looped around confused me. Was I doing this because there was proof that I'd already done it? Or I was doing it because I was, period. And if I didn't, maybe someone who resembled me would or Caravaggio would add my features to the model before him. Who knew what the answer was?

The light in the room grew dim, shadows blooming from the corners. Hours had passed and I hadn't tried to find Mom, hadn't helped Bruno. Tomorrow, I told myself. For sure.

"Enough for today," Caravaggio announced, throwing down his brushes. "Time to clear our heads with some good wine and cheap women."

"And time for me to get back to Del Monte's." What would Dad say if I went to some bar, even if I was with a famous artist?

"Don't leave us yet!" Caravaggio protested. "I can at least buy you supper for your trouble."

"I was happy to sit for you." I stretched my stiff neck and shoulders.

"Come with us," Giovanni urged, touching my arm.

My heart flipped in my chest. I nodded, and the three of us made our way downstairs and out into the gathering dusk.

I hadn't walked around Rome at night before. Torches blazed outside some buildings, but mostly the city was quickly swallowed in inky darkness. The stars overhead glittered brightly, turning the sky into an ocean of brilliant lights. The streets weren't as crowded as during the day, but plenty of people were still out. Most of them seemed to be heading for the same place Caravaggio led us to, an inn with the sign of a grinning dark face wrapped in a turban.

"Welcome to the Moor of the Magdalen!" Caravaggio said, bowing low and sweeping his arm out in front of him in an expansive gesture. "My friends should already be here, or they'll be here soon, or they'll be here later. In any case, we're here now!"

We shoved our way through the crowded room, sour with the smell of beer and sweat, pungent with garlic and onion. I couldn't imagine eating anything in such a strong stench—it would be like swallowing Malcolm's stinky sock pile.

A few men wore fine velvets like Caravaggio, a few wore filthy rags, but most were dressed in between.

I guessed they were blacksmiths, cartwrights, butchers. The same kind of working-class guys you'd find in a modern bar. Women dressed in low-cut blouses flitted from man to man, drumming up their own kind of business, but no women were there as customers. I felt not just out of my time, but completely out of place.

Caravaggio sat down at one of the long tables with a few free stools. Giovanni settled next to him. I wavered, not sure I should stay. I wasn't helping Bruno here, but I wanted a little more time with Giovanni. An hour couldn't hurt, I told myself. Maybe I'd even learn something useful.

There wasn't a menu or anything that looked like a restaurant, but Caravaggio told a scruffy-looking man what he wanted. The room rumbled with loud conversations, and I had to yell over the din.

"So," I bellowed. "I hear from Del Monte that his friend, Bruno, is in prison for heresy!"

Caravaggio shrugged. "It's easy to get on the wrong side of the Inquisition, but you'd have to be a fool to be condemned. Take me, for example. Some cardinal has to approve my sketches before I can paint. But since I don't do sketches, all they can judge is the underpainting, the way I block out the composition in lights and darks. Foolishness, all of it!"

"Have you ever had to change something because they didn't like it?"

"No! And I wouldn't if they begged me!" Caravaggio gulped his wine. Would he end up in prison for heresy like Bruno? Was I supposed to save both of them?

"Ah, there's Onorio!" The door had opened and a gust blew in a group of four men, all clamoring for Caravaggio. His painter friends, I guessed. They shouldered their way through the throng and took places next to the artist. One glare from the man Caravaggio called Onorio was enough to send a benchful of people off to the corner.

Onorio had a polished look to him. A silver sword hung at his waist. Even his curled mustache looked expensive. His clothes and manner were clearly better than the average customer's.

"The nobility is here to give this place some class!" he swaggered, somehow managing to take up far more space than a normal person would, all broad shoulders and straddling legs. I'd seen Caravaggio switch from braggart to kind young man. Now it was the opposite. Onorio seemed to bring out the blowhard in the artist.

Which meant the end of my chance to get any information about Bruno. The talk turned quickly to other painters—the good, the bad, and the hacks. Mostly they made fun of artists with weak colors, limp figures, and soulless, empty images. I tried to listen, but I felt miserable, thinking what they would say about my own drawing. I checked that my sketchbook was safely hidden in my pocket, praying they'd never see anything in it.

This didn't seem like a group that'd be interested in theories about the earth's movements, so the chance of hearing anything helpful seemed slim. And the longer I was with them, the more uncomfortable I felt. I'd often been around boys. After all, I had an older brother, but this was different, kind of like how I imagined a frat party would be. Loud and rude and coarse, with plenty of swearing, belching, and swilling of wine. Caravaggio was the loudest and rudest of all, but even angelic Giovanni joined in. When he started flirting with one of the women selling her services, I felt sick to my stomach.

I'd made up my mind to leave when the sallow-faced man brought two plates of artichokes for the table.

"Which are cooked in olive oil and which in butter?" Caravaggio demanded.

"Smell them and then you'll know," said the man sullenly.

"Smell them yourself!" roared Caravaggio, standing up in a fit of rage. He grabbed the plates from the man and hurled them at him. "What do they smell like to you?"

The man cowered and tried to ward off the thrown crockery, but not quickly enough. One plate caught him on the cheek, and the other flew over his shoulder.

"Ayyyyy!" he howled, burned or cut or both. He ran into the kitchen, cursing loudly.

"Now you've done it!" Onorio said. "You can't go a week without getting arrested for some stupid nonsense! When will you learn to control that temper?"

"The wretch deserved it!" Caravaggio scowled.

"Let's go!" Giovanni yelled. "The fool's calling for the sbirri. They'll be here soon!"

The door flew open and six men burst in. Giovanni turned pale. Caravaggio glowered. Onorio looked fed up. The men didn't look like police except for the red cape that Morton had pointed out to me. So these were the sbirri? How had the police heard so fast?

If they had looked like modern cops, I would have been more afraid. But they didn't and that's what gave me the idea. I picked up the pitcher of wine and threw it at one of the sbirri as they headed to our table. "Leave him alone!" I shouted.

The pitcher glanced off the man's barrel chest, smashing onto the floor. "Get him!" he bellowed.

"You again!" another one snarled at Caravaggio.

Before I could move, my arms were wrenched behind my back, the sbirro's face so close to mine that I couldn't avoid his rancid breath, like he'd chewed on a long-dead rat. "You'll pay for that!" he barked.

Icy terror gripped me. Just because he didn't have a uniform, a badge, a gun didn't mean he couldn't beat me up. Now I'd really done it! I tried to keep myself from shivering as I was frog-marched out the door into the cool night air and down the street to a gloomy tall building. And that's how I was thrown into a Roman prison.

February 8, 1600

HOME SWEET ROME

I was a good kid. I'd never gotten detention, never been sent to the principal's office, never even been grounded by my parents. And here I was in a dark, dank, smelly cell, more dungeon than jail.

At least I wasn't alone. Caravaggio had also been arrested.

"Why did you assault the sbirri?" he asked after the jailor clanged the door shut and we were alone. "You don't seem like the type and you hadn't drunk a drop."

I couldn't explain the real reason, so I asked my own question. "Why did you attack the waiter?"

"He deserved it!" Caravaggio studied me as if I'd grown a mustache overnight. "Were you defending me? You hardly know me."

I wondered if I should tell him the truth. Or should I pretend I was some kind of hero—a stupid one, but a hero all the same?

"I admire your talent," I finally grumbled, hoping that was explanation enough.

"You don't seem hotheaded like me." Caravaggio grinned, clearly proud of his temper. "There's some other reason."

"Actually, there is," I decided to admit. "I'm looking for a prisoner here. This seemed like the best way to talk to him."

Caravaggio roared with laughter. "Good luck finding him! Tor di Nona is huge. And even if you do find him, how do you get yourself out of here afterward?"

Panic surged through me. I hadn't planned that far in advance. Throwing the pitcher had been a quick impulse. It had seemed like a good idea at the time. I wondered how many people who found themselves in trouble had thought the same thing.

"How will you get out?" I asked. "Since we were arrested together, wouldn't we be released at the same time?"

"Del Monte will get me out in the morning. He always does." Caravaggio settled himself down on the filthy straw pallet in the corner, unconcerned about lice, bedbugs, or whatever nasty germs lurked in its disgustingness. Within minutes he was snoring.

Caravaggio obviously wasn't worried. But I wasn't a famous painter and I didn't have powerful friends and patrons. Maybe Mom could get me out. Or Morton. If they knew I was here. I slumped down against the cold stone wall, exhausted. Or maybe one of the stones here, in this cell, was a touchstone.

But I needed to be here. I had a job to do. Then I could figure out how to get out. The door was heavy, solid wood, the walls all stone, but there was a small barred window next to the door and another one high up on the opposite wall, letting in a thin stream of moonlight.

"Bruno!" I called through the bars by the door. "I'm a friend of Del Monte's. Can you hear me?"

There was no answer except for Caravaggio's rhythmic snores.

"Are you there? Bruno!" I screamed. Had I gotten myself arrested for nothing? "BRUNO!"

"Shut up!" an angry voice barked. "There's no Bruno here!"

"Do you know him? Do you know where I can find him?"

"NOOOOO!" the voice roared. "Now let me sleep!"

Caravaggio looked up blearily. "Look, if you want to find Bruno, there's really only one way. You have to pay the guard to let you visit him. That's how things are done inside prison and out. Money opens all doors."

"But I don't have any money." I dug my hands into my pockets. My sketchbook, pen, Mom's note, and a couple of crumpled euros, all completely worthless in the sixteenth century.

Caravaggio threw a few coins at me. "Good thing you got

arrested with me. Now tell the guard you've got something for him."

I grabbed the coins, glinting dully in the filthy straw. "Thank you, really, thank you!" The painter surprised me—throwing a plate of artichokes one minute, money the next. He was clearly a good person to have as a friend, a terrible one to have as an enemy.

"Guard!" I shouted through the barred window near the door. "I can pay for your services! I can pay!"

Money really did talk. Two minutes later, the guard, a skinny old man with a shiny bald head, was outside the door. "What do you want?" he asked greedily.

"I need to speak to another prisoner here—Giordano Bruno." I held a coin through the bars. "Here's for your troubles."

The old man snatched the money in his long, bony fingers. "That's enough to get you into the same cell as Bruno. What will you pay to get back out of it?" He laughed hoarsely.

I offered another coin, hoping it would be enough. I didn't want to give up the third coin in case I needed it. How did I know I could trust the old man?

The guard nodded, taking the money. He chose a key from the large ring tied to his waist and inserted it into the door.

"Are we leaving so soon, Francesco?" Caravaggio asked, grinning. I wondered how often he got locked up, to know the guard by name.

"You're staying right where you are!" the old man barked.

"You'll get out in the morning, same as always. Now it's this young lad's turn."

"Thank you," I turned to whisper to Caravaggio. I followed Francesco down the corridor, dimly lit by the torch he held, then up a narrow winding staircase. I hurried behind the guard, afraid I'd lose him and be trapped in inky blackness. After the stairs, the damp stone hall wasn't as dark as thin moonlight leaked in from high barred windows every so often. Still, the place was creepy. Maybe I should have thought of escaping, but all I could think of was that I had to find Bruno, that this was important.

We passed several wooden doors, and I couldn't help wondering who or what was behind them. Horrible instruments of torture, the kind the word "Inquisition" conjures up? The infamous rack, the evil thumbscrew? I was trying not to imagine anything, to focus on the bright torch, when Francesco stopped in front of a door. The guard sorted through his thick ring of keys, the metal clanking echoing on the stones. The door opened with a groan, clearly unaccustomed to movement.

"I'll fetch you in the morning," Francesco rasped, pushing me into the cell and slamming the door behind me. The dull thud filled me with dread, even though I was where I wanted to be. At least I thought I wanted to be here in this large chilly cell, the air dank and moldy.

"Who wakes a tired, old man trying to sleep and lose himself in pleasant dreams?" a voice quavered in the darkness.

"I'm Marco, and I'm looking for Giordano Bruno," I said.

"Then your search is at an end." The voice sighed.

A rat scurried by and I yelped, startled, but even the nasty rodent couldn't dim the triumph I felt. I'd found Bruno! Now if I could just convince him to admit to the Inquisition that he'd made a mistake.

"Bruno, I'm here to warn you—you must recant. If you don't, not only will you be killed, but all your writings will be destroyed. All your work will be for nothing!"

"Who are you? And why should you care?"

"I'm a friend, a fellow scholar. I know about your theories and you're absolutely right, but being right won't keep you alive. Just say what the Inquisition wants to hear and you'll be able to keep on writing."

"Even if I wanted to, I couldn't." Bruno sounded defeated. "They want me punished and silenced."

"If you recant, they won't condemn you—that's what Del Monte says."

"You don't understand. You can't understand. Since I must die, it's better for it to be by the Inquisition's hand."

"But why do you have to die?" He sounded so sad and lonely. "I've heard some of your theories, not just about the earth orbiting the sun, but about parallel worlds and other times, about atoms. I think you're right. Your ideas are important, so isn't it better to tell the Inquisitors what they want to hear and go on writing? Don't you want to keep your ideas alive?"

"It was a mistake, all of it."

"No, it wasn't! And there are other people who agree with you, men of science like Galileo."

"Galileo! He took my post, the one at the University of Pisa. They hired him to head the school of mathematics instead of me. Ah, well, maybe it's better that way…"

"Why better? You're both brilliant men. You both deserve the position."

"No, he truly deserves it because his studies come from observation, from his own reasoning."

"And yours don't? Where else would they come from?"

"I'm a thief, that's what I am. And that's why I'll be punished. I stole ideas from others." Bruno's voice was stronger now but still flat with sorrow.

"What do you mean, thief? I thought all writers borrow from other authors. All scientists build on other scientists' work."

"That's not stealing!"

"Exactly my point," I said, encouraged that Bruno seemed angry more than mournful, even though he was mad at me.

"You can't understand!"

All I was doing was making him really not like me. But I couldn't give up, so I tried again, hoping I wasn't sticking my foot in my mouth. "You don't mean copying exactly what other people wrote, do you?"

"I wasn't taking credit for other people's work. I was keeping it alive, giving it a future. At least, that's what I thought I was doing."

I thought about the book of his I'd copied. It described atoms, which Del Monte said were an ancient Greek idea. Was that what he meant? Then it came to me in a flash—maybe Bruno didn't mean he'd learned from other people's books. Maybe he'd learned from other people! Maybe he was a time traveler, too!

Which obviously wasn't something I could ask without sounding crazy. Instead I said, "Bruno, I think I know what you mean. Did you study geometry with Euclid in ancient Greece? Did you meet Pythagoras? Maybe even Lucretius?"

There was a long silence. He could have thought I meant their books. Or he could understand what I was hinting at. I waited. The minutes felt heavy around me, weighing me down. Such a strange thing Time was—sometimes fast, sometimes slow, whirling around me, sucking me into one time, spitting me out in another, this happening because that had already happened, but that happening because this was about to. It was all a big muddle. I shook my head, trying to clear my mind. I needed to focus on the here and now, not on Time itself.

"I know about other times," I dared to say finally. "I know about touchstones."

There, I'd done it. Either he thought I was crazy or he knew exactly what I meant.

"You're not just a scholar, are you? What time are you from?"

So he was a time traveler! I wondered if Mom knew, if that was why she wanted to save him. "I'm from a time that knows you're right and that wants to help you, that wants to keep your ideas alive."

"They aren't my ideas—they belong to humanity! I thought I was doing good," Bruno sobbed. "I learned so much from them. I just wanted to share their knowledge. I meant no harm! I wasn't changing the past any more than anyone else. I was simply bringing their theories into my own time."

I thought about that. Many of the writings of ancient scholars were lost in the so-called Dark Ages. Bruno was only recovering what would be found eventually anyway. Better sooner than later, better more light in the darkness.

"You're right," I told him. "So all you need to do is recant to appease the Inquisition."

"You think I'm right, but the Watchers don't. The chief Inquisitor, Bellarmine, has made it clear he doesn't want to condemn me. He's told me all I need to say is that my ideas are wild speculation, not based in any science at all. But the Watcher, he told me that I've interfered with Time by bringing back ancient theories and for that I must die. If not by the hand of the Inquisition, then they'll arrange something, something that might not fit in with my natural time at all."

An icy chill gripped me. Did the Watchers want to kill Mom, too?

"So you understand, I must be executed." Bruno's low, sad voice broke into my thoughts. "I've tried to find a touchstone, to flee, but I've been here for years now. There's no hope."

"No touchstones here?" I tried to push down the panic swelling inside me.

"If I were wiser, I wouldn't need them," Bruno said. "All potentials exist side by side. The problem is that we don't see the possibilities. We don't think we have any control over them, but we do."

"Then why can't you wish yourself into another time, another place?"

"Because I would need pure positive thought for that."

"You mean, you just need to want something badly enough?" That didn't seem hard to me, kind of like Dorothy clicking her ruby slippers and wishing to go back to Kansas.

"That would be easy! But you need to believe something, really believe it. Most of us have doubts, hesitations. We may have a layer of positive thought, but underneath it, there's fear." Bruno stood up, his shadow looming out of the darkness.

"The world isn't independent of our experience of it. Our intent changes the past as much as the future. We just aren't aware of it. We aren't controlling it." He shook his head sadly. "That's why it's foolish for the Watchers to punish me, to think I'm guilty of changing the past. We all are! In a million tiny ways we're totally unconscious of."

His words reminded me of a movie I'd watched with Malcolm, a film about quantum physics that said there are an infinite number of possibilities in front of us, but we don't know how to see them. That matter isn't a thing but a possibility, and that it's our perceptions that affect reality—past, present, and future. Was that what Bruno was describing? Was he a brilliant physicist long before physics was a recognized science? And did that mean time travel was one of those possibilities, one of those things we could control simply with thought?

Bruno was describing how souls move from body to body, from animals to people, from people to beasts, but I couldn't follow him. I was too distracted trying to figure out the physics of time travel. If I was smarter, I'd be able to control things!

"That's a hard theory to believe," I said, trying to grasp the implications. He made reality—and time—sound like clay, there to be shaped by us however we wanted.

"No harder than thinking that the earth orbits the sun," he responded. "For most people now, that's absurd, impossible.

But you know it to be true. Every time has its own assumptions, its own blind spots." Bruno slumped back down against the wall. "Ideas are powerful, the most powerful things of all. That's why there's an Inquisition—the Church understands that the real threat doesn't come from armies but from thoughts."

He sounded so modern, not like an old-fashioned scholar at all. He could have been talking about the dangers of propaganda, the importance of a free press. I remembered the book we'd read in school last year, *Brave New World*, where the government controlled the people by controlling every bit of information. Bruno was right, which meant he could save himself.

"You can believe your way out of here!" I urged. "You've traveled through the centuries, and you've met so many brilliant people. You have to have faith in yourself!"

"I've tried for years, believe me," he said. "But I can't. Maybe you can—you need to find a way out of here, too. Otherwise you'll rot in here forever or be sent to the galleys, rowing your way to a slow, tortuous death."

"Don't worry about me. I'll figure something out," I lied. I had no plans, no ideas, no hope. I'd come here to save Bruno and all I'd done was trap myself.

There was a long silence. Then Bruno spoke again.

"It was worth it. To learn what I learned, to see what I saw, to meet the brilliant men I dreamed of. I gained knowledge worth dying for."

"You were fortunate then," I blurted out. I wasn't ready to die, but if that's what was going to happen, then I wanted to learn as much as possible, the way Bruno had.

"There are so many possibilities!" Bruno sighed. "So many better endings my life must have in those other worlds."

"Then it's not so sad to die in this one, is it?" I offered. "And if you believe your soul will be reborn, death is a kind of beginning." I wasn't sure I believed this at all, but I hoped the idea would give him some comfort.

"You know, Galileo thinks that, too. I'm the one punished for heresy, but he has some of the same beliefs." A note of bitterness crept into Bruno's voice.

"Like the earth rotating around the sun?" That was the most famous one. The one that would get Galileo in trouble in the end.

"Yes, we've both read Copernicus. But I've actually met him." For a moment, he sounded proud, not defeated.

"Tell me what he was like," I said, "what they all were like, the brilliant people you met."

"Of them all, the philosophers, the artists, the writers, my favorite was Aristophanes, the Greek playwright. His satires were biting and funny in equal measure. He used laughter to take the sting out of his criticism. Which somehow made his barbs all the sharper."

"That sounds like you in the book I read."

Bruno was a scientist and a philosopher, a mathematician and comedy writer, so many things at once. He saw the world in such broad terms that I could feel the walls of the prison drop away as he spoke, describing other people, other histories. I tried to follow everything he said, to understand the fluidity of Time, like a river you could walk through and find yourself in a different place at each crossing, but the idea was too much for me to hold in my head.

What I grasped was an impression of the world full of glinting lights, a million futures, a zillion possibilities, an infinite number of ways forward and back. It was all so perfectly beautiful, so incredibly ingenious, like the way you can find math in nature—from the swirls of seashells to the spines of pinecones. When dawn streamed in the high window, I hadn't moved at all, but I felt like I'd time-traveled in a totally different way.

The guard clanged open the door down the hall, and Bruno stopped talking mid-sentence. My time was up and I hadn't accomplished anything. I shivered in dread.

"Time to go!" the bald old man called, unlocking the cell. He glared at Bruno. "Not you."

Now that it was light, I could see Bruno's face. His curly hair was salt and pepper, like the stubble on his cheeks and his scraggly beard, but his deep-set eyes and broad forehead gave him a noble look. He locked his eyes on mine.

"Tell your mother I'm fine. I'll be fine. I know what I'm doing."

"Mom? You know Mom?" I stammered, stunned and terrified. What kind of trouble had she gotten herself into? Was she next on the Watchers' list?

"Come on!" Francesco snarled. "Or stay here the rest of your life. Your choice."

"What do you know?" I asked Bruno, stumbling toward the door on stiff legs. "What should I do?"

He waved a tired hand at me. "Go in peace. Be at peace. I am."

The guard shoved me out of the cell and slammed the door shut. I followed him numbly. I could have talked to Bruno about Mom, but I hadn't known to ask! I clenched my fists, furious at myself. We'd talked about the nature of the universe, of time, of human potential, when I could have found out why Mom was trapped in the past and how to get her out. I'd wasted my time with Bruno, and now I was stuck in prison when I needed to see Mom, to tell her there was no point being here, no possibility of saving Bruno. We should just go home, the both of us!

Francesco wound his way back down the stone stairs, back along the gloomy corridor, back to the cell where Caravaggio waited. The jailor opened the door and shoved me inside. This cell was smaller than Bruno's but no more welcoming. In the thin morning light I could make out marks gouged into the wall, someone's way of counting the miserable days.

The thud of the door must have woken the painter. Caravaggio stretched and yawned as if he'd spent the night in his own comfortable bed. "Ciao, Marco. I'll see if Del Monte can get you freed as well, but I warn you, he's busy fretting about that Bruno fellow you were asking about." Caravaggio combed the straw out of his hair with his fingers. "How was your visit? Anything I should mention to Del Monte?"

"He's a remarkable man," I said, trying to collect my thoughts. If thoughts were as powerful as Bruno said, why did I feel so weak?

"So I've heard." Caravaggio frowned. "It's all too easy to run afoul of the Inquisition. They want to control what's said, what's written, what's painted. As if they know the truth about what's holy! All they really care about is power. Which means curiosity, learning, exploring—those are all threats to them."

Bruno was right—the Inquisition was a kind of thought police, as if you couldn't be a good Catholic and have a questioning mind.

The door creaked open. It was Francesco again. "Your turn, pretty boy!" He gestured toward Caravaggio. "Until the next time."

"Just in case." The painter slipped some coins into my hand.

I nodded, silent, trying not to cry.

The door shut and I was left alone with chilly stone walls, a nasty straw pallet, and rats. Plenty of rats.

February 11, 1600

If reality really could be controlled by our thoughts, I would have melted the prison walls and walked out into the cold winter day. But I wasn't a brilliant physicist and I couldn't control much of anything.

Days passed. I touched every single stone in the cell, no matter how slimy, desperate to find a touchstone. I added my scratches to the marks already on the wall. I closed my eyes and tried to think my way out. I cried until I was too exhausted for any more tears. And I ate wormy gruel even though I swore I wouldn't touch the filthy stuff. How would I ever escape?

You know those stories about kidnapped people and how they stay sane by reciting the alphabet or any poems they've memorized? Let me say, that didn't help at all. Instead, I sang every stupid camp song I could think of. I had long conversations with Mom, Dad, and Malcolm.

But mostly I drew. I still had my sketchbook with me, and I drew everything I could remember from when we first got to Rome. From the ragwort to Bruno's face. I thought about what Malcolm had said, that he thought I was talented. If I ever get out of here, I promised myself, I'll show him these sketches. He'll get to see sixteenth-century Rome himself.

The sun was high in the small window on the third day, and I could hear many footsteps, when the door opened again. Two soldiers shoved past Francesco, each grabbing me by an arm.

"What's going on?" I yelled, trying to twist out of their grips. "I'm innocent!" I'd forgotten why I'd been thrown in prison in the first place—oh yeah, the wine jug, the sbirri, the plate of artichokes.

"You're getting out of here!" snapped one soldier.

"You should be happy about that!" sneered the other, pushing me out of the cell. I bumped into a filthy man with matted hair and crazy eyes, another prisoner. There were a dozen of us, plus as many soldiers.

"Where are we going?" I whispered to a boy about my age.

"To the galleys!" he hissed back, his eyes round with fright.

"What's that?" I asked, though clearly the answer wasn't good.

"Ships! We'll be slaves, chained to the oars and made to row until we die. They might as well kill us right now!"

I'd thrown a jug at a policeman and I was sentenced to slavery for that? I hadn't even had a trial! Could I get word to Del

Monte? Could Morton save me? Maybe I could find a touchstone. The soldiers hadn't bothered to tie my hands, so that was my only chance.

We stumbled out of the prison gate into the daylight, momentarily blinded by the bright winter sun. I gulped in the cool, fresh 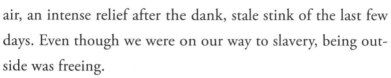 air, an intense relief after the dank, stale stink of the last few days. Even though we were on our way to slavery, being outside was freeing.

I had to find a touchstone before we got to the ships and disappear my way out of the punishment. The soldiers walked in front, alongside, and behind us, using their sharp halberds to poke anybody who stumbled on weakened legs. How could I get past them? I hadn't eaten or slept well for so long that I couldn't count on outrunning anyone. I'd never been very fast even when I was well-rested.

You think you can bear anything, that you'll be defiant and fight your way out of terrible situations. Then when they actually happen, you find out how easy it is to give in, how hard it is to stay determined and strong. I thought of Bruno, how he didn't deserve to die, how I didn't deserve to die, and somehow that gave me more energy. There had to be a chance for an escape, and when I saw it, I'd take it.

We were walking toward the Tiber River, where the boats waited for their slave crew. We were almost at the bridge when a man pushing a cart piled high with onions slipped and tipped his cart. I didn't understand how something so heavy could fall over, but there wasn't time to figure that out as onions rolled under, around, over everything.

"My onions!" The man pushed though the soldiers, through the prisoners, racing to collect as many as he could. The starving prisoners grabbed the onions, too, some even biting into them right away. The soldiers tried to keep control of both us and the onions, yelling at the merchant for being such a clumsy idiot.

"Out of my way!" The onion man shoved me hard. My hip crackled where he'd touched me and I recognized the disguised figure, the voice. It was Mom!

I wanted to grab her, to hug her, but I knew what she was doing. I took the chance she gave me and sprinted over the bridge, ducking into the first side street I saw, turning corners, twisting through the alleys. I ran until my legs burned and my lungs ached. Long after anybody could have been following me, I kept on running, pushed on by panic.

Careening wildly through the streets, I found myself back at St. Peter's. Here, finally, I stopped to catch my breath, my legs feeling wobbly from sprinting. There in the piazza in front of the great dome was an obelisk. And on the ground around it, the symbols of the zodiac. It was both obelisk and meridian, marker and sundial.

Relief surged through me. It could be a touchstone. I thought about what Bruno had said—how our perceptions shape reality. Could I make the obelisk a touchstone by believing it was one?

"Halt!" a gruff voice yelled. The soldiers had found me. I pushed down the terror rising inside me and focused on the obelisk. I forced myself to think of Dad and Malcolm as I reached out and touched the carved marker, looking to see if Mom was behind me. But all I saw was smoke billowing around me, sucking up marble, stone, and dust, spitting out earth, wind, and fire. I was spinning in a haze of colors, of dawns and dusks, starry nights and blazing days.

July 7

When my head stopped spinning, I was back in my jeans. I gulped in the fresh, modern air. I was safe! Now my legs really gave way, partly from exhaustion, partly in intense relief. I sat sprawled on the pavement and tipped my face up to the sun, gloriously happy to be here, now, in this moment.

I just sat there like that, savoring the light breeze in my hair, the warmth of the day, the chatter of tourists as they passed by. What had Bruno said? Something about our perceptions shaping our world, our future? I tried to hold on to what he had told me, but it was all so complicated, and the dark days in the prison had dulled the brightness of his words.

At least I'd seen Mom. I hadn't saved Bruno, but I knew she was okay. And maybe, just maybe, I'd learned how to make a stone a touchstone. Either that, or I was plain lucky.

I headed to our hotel, eager to see Dad and Malcolm, to hold them tight. I walked quickly, drinking in the rumbling of cars, the buzz of tourists talking, giddy with happiness to be back in the right time. In a foreign city, surrounded by strangers, I felt deeply at home. I belonged here in this time. The edge of anxiety that buzzed through me whenever I time-traveled was gone.

Suddenly I understood why Bruno was willing to die under the Inquisition. If the choice was that or be killed by the Watchers while time-traveling, it was far better to finish your days in the time when you belonged. There was a rightness to it, a comfort even in the face of death.

When I got back to the hotel, Dad and Malcolm were waiting for me.

"What happened?" Dad jumped up from the bed as soon as I opened the door. "Did you see Mom?"

I wrapped my arms around him, squeezing hard the way I had when I was little. Then I hugged Malcolm, who gave me a who-are-you look. That made Dad even more worried. "What happened?" he asked again.

I took a deep breath and explained everything, from posing for Caravaggio to getting myself thrown in prison. Dad didn't interrupt me, and neither did Malcolm. They just looked more and more worried as I told my story.

"You could have been killed!" Dad said when I was finished. "That's it! You're done time-traveling!"

"You forget I don't have a choice," I said. "And Mom saved me. It was okay."

"She barely saved you. And who's saving her? What if that Watcher tries to punish Mom the way she's punishing Bruno?" Dad said exactly what I'd been afraid of.

"You know, if you don't touch anything, any stones at all, you'll be safe," Malcolm suggested. "You can control this time-travel stuff more than you think."

"Only sometimes," I said. "Usually I can't. Sometimes the touchstone pulls me in, like a kind of powerful magnet. Besides, I have to help Mom!"

"Not if it means hurting you!" Dad said. "She wouldn't want that. She has to be doing this to protect you, to change something in our future that scares her. There's no other reason she'd break the rules."

A faraway look crept over Malcolm's face, like he was time-traveling himself or trying to figure out some kind of difficult puzzle. "What if that's part of the problem?" he said. "What if Time is like a Möbius strip, folding over itself so you can't tell what's cause and what's effect?"

"What do you mean?" I asked.

"I mean, what if Mom went back in time to try to stop

139

something terrible from happening in the future, so the Watcher chases Mom and tries to punish her, and that punishment ends up being whatever the terrible thing is that Mom is trying to stop from happening in the first place."

I tried to follow Malcolm's logic.

If Event X is to be stopped, Y must make Event Z happen in the past, but by making Event Z, Y has committed a time crime and must be punished, which is Event X.

"But that's a paradox!" I blurted out. "It makes no sense!"

"And then the Watcher should be punished, too, because she's also changing the past by interfering with what Mom does," Dad said, his forehead wrinkling in concentration. Was this as confusing for him as it was for me? "Basically anyone who does anything in the past changes it. The only safe thing to do is observe, and none of you—not Mom, not the Watcher, not you, and certainly not Bruno—is doing that."

"Bruno said that we all change the time we're in, even when we observe. He said that our perceptions affect reality, that time is more fluid than we think it is." I sighed, suddenly exhausted. "He said we're just like the people in the Inquisition believing that the sun orbits the earth. We're blinded by our own preconceptions."

"He sounds like an amazing person!" Malcolm said wistfully. "You get to meet the coolest people!"

"We've been doing some research on Bruno while you were gone," Dad added. "He was an interesting thinker. Science wasn't a separate area of study in the Renaissance. It was part of philosophy, of understanding the world. Bruno had an incredible ability to describe the universe and our own actions in it as cause and effect, just like you're saying now."

"What's really fascinating is that he sounds like a physicist—a quantum physicist, the area where science becomes philosophy." Malcolm sounded excited. "For someone who traveled into the past, he was actually like a man from the future, way ahead of his time!"

"I wish I could have saved him. There must be something I can do."

"We'll figure this out. I'm sure we will." Dad's words were confident but his tone wasn't. "How about we forget about the past for now and enjoy the present?" Dad hugged me tight. "And no touching anything, okay?"

"Yeah." Malcolm shuffled his feet nervously. "There's so much to see, and you haven't had a chance to really do much."

"Have you?" I asked suspiciously. "I thought you were waiting for me here."

"You were gone for hours this time. We're not going to waste the day in a hotel room." Malcolm sounded defensive, but that's exactly what I thought they'd done.

"You did fun stuff without me?" I tried not to whine, but there it was, an annoying snivel in my voice. I rotted in prison while they ate pizza and saw amazing ruins.

"Dad had to take pictures for his book after all, and I wanted to see Nero's Golden Palace, the Palatine Hill, the Colosseum. Did you know you can actually go inside Emperor Augustus' house?"

"Do you have to gloat about it?"

"I'm not gloating! You get to see all these amazing things in amazing times. You can't begrudge me a small taste of what you get!"

"Mira," Dad interrupted. "Be fair to your brother. We can see all those things again with you, but you can't expect us to do nothing but worry and work in Internet cafés while you time-travel."

Of course, I couldn't. But I was hurt that they'd done all these interesting things without me. Which was probably how Malcolm felt about what I got to do.

"Okay, you're right. But I thought about you this time, and I made sketches like you suggested." If I could survive days in a Roman prison, I could endure Malcolm criticizing my drawings.

"You did? For me?" Malcolm looked ridiculously pleased. "I'd love to see them."

I handed him my sketchbook, but I couldn't watch him leaf

through the pages. I wasn't that strong! Instead I hid in the bathroom, soaking in a good hot shower.

When I came out, Dad and Malcolm were sitting on one of the beds, still poring over the sketchbook.

"These are really good, Mira!" my brother said, not one hint of teasing in his voice.

"You've inherited your grandfather's talent." Dad glowed with pride.

"They're just scratches," I shrugged, embarrassed, but I was proud, too. "Now do I get to see some of this city that you've already seen? Like Nero's Golden Palace. That sounds cool."

"Of course," Dad agreed. "But first I thought we'd go to the market in Campo de' Fiori to get stuff for a picnic lunch. Then we can see Nero's palace or go to the Vatican Library and see what else we can learn about Bruno and the Inquisition."

"Sounds good," I said, torn between being an ordinary tourist and helping Mom. "I think Mom was doing something at the Vatican, trying to convince the chief Inquisitor, Cardinal Bellarmine, to leave Bruno alone. Maybe she left a clue for us. Or a note."

We wound our way

through the streets to the Campo de' Fiori, a big piazza near the southern bend of the Tiber. Just as Dad had said, stands filled the space, selling everything from olives to aprons, cheeses to fresh fish, still gasping for air in buckets of water.

In the center of the piazza stood a bronze statue of a hooded monk holding a big book. It was a dark, brooding figure in the middle of the market's hustle and bustle. Its somber shadow cast a pall over tourists licking gelato and eating slices of pizza. Malcolm was picking though peaches, Dad was buying bread, and all I could think about was the sculpture and the sadness that emanated from it like a gray mist.

I inched closer and read the plaque under the figure. As I realized who it was, I couldn't help shivering. It was Bruno, and the statue marked the place where he'd been burned at the stake, February 17, 1600.

"Want a peach?" Malcolm offered.

I stared at him. "It's Bruno!"

"No, it's a peach." Malcolm looked confused.

"Not that! The statue!" I looked up at the sculpture. This was the man who'd talked to me about souls moving from one person to another, from one time to another, about the earth orbiting the sun, about people's thoughts shaping reality.

And even though we'd just talked about how I shouldn't touch stones anymore, I couldn't help it. The plaque called to me. I leaned out and gingerly traced with my finger Bruno's name, cast in bronze. An intense heat shot out from the base, and flames wrapped themselves around the statue. The cobbled streets buckled like in an earthquake, while chasms zigzagged across the ground, swallowing up merchants, stands, tourists, everything in a whirl of black and red.

February 17, 1600

When the dust settled and I could see again, I was still in Campo de' Fiori, but the market stalls were gone. Instead there were thickset men in leather aprons, toothless women with dirt-smudged skirts, soldiers holding pikes and lances, and monks in shadowy hoods, a crowd of people cheering and jeering. And in the place of the sculpture, there was a man, a real man, tied to a stake with flames already reaching up to his chest. I felt sick to my stomach, but I couldn't tear my eyes away. It was Bruno.

He writhed in agony. I wanted to throw water on the flames, to free him from the stake, but I was horribly helpless.

"Bruno!" I screamed, tears streaming down my face. I needed him to know I was there. That he wasn't alone in this nightmare. "Bruno!"

He turned and found me with his eyes. He looked like he wanted to shout something, but his mouth was blocked with a wooden gag, a last twist of cruelty. The smell of scorched flesh was nauseating, but the crowd cheered as if they were at a sporting event, not a murder. They were all excited to see the spectacle of a public execution. Mom had to be in the crowd. Maybe the Watcher, too.

I had to get away, it was all too sickening, but I locked eyes with Bruno one last time. He was still alive, and I swear he recognized me. He stared at me in a way I'll never forget, fierce and proud. Then he closed his eyes and went limp against the ropes that bound him.

"Good-bye, Bruno," I murmured. I turned to push my way through the crowd. People were packed together tighter than in Times Square on New Year's Eve. I had to elbow into a skinny man with a bulging goiter and shove aside a woman with hairs bristling out of her warty chin. I squeezed past a young man in an elegant cape and hat, relieved that not everyone around me was dirty or ugly or both, but when I turned for a closer look at the gentleman, I gasped. It was the Watcher, Madame L. She reached out to grab me, but I edged behind a fat, smelly monk, leaving her with a handful of the man's paunch.

"I told you to stay away!" She seethed, shoving the startled monk aside.

"Leave my mother alone!" I demanded, suddenly furious. "You killed Bruno—isn't that enough?"

"I haven't touched your mother. And Bruno got what he deserved. Just be careful you don't earn the same fate!" The woman shoved me down a side alley. "Now get out of here—and tell your mother I mean it! Bruno's all the proof she needs." She melted back into the crowd, a sinister smile playing on her beautiful lips.

I stumbled away, scared and sickened. How could I stop the Watcher? I thought of Bruno, of his faith in positive thinking. If I really wanted, could I control any of this? Was I strong and smart enough for that? Focused enough?

I needed desperately to go home, back to my own time. Dad and Malcolm would help me. I knew they would. All around me the faces of ordinary people looked like evil demons now, all cheering on Bruno's torture. The man pushing the wheelbarrow, the woman carrying water, even the boy with baskets of bread—they were all deformed with ugly, sneering faces.

I touched walls frantically, wishing hard for the future, but none of them were touchstones. Then I saw it—a strange statue in the corner of a small piazza. It was clearly an ancient ruin, dragged from the Forum probably, a classical head and torso set on a broken column. On the figure itself, on the column, on the wall behind it, pieces of paper had been stuck up somehow. It was like an old-fashioned community newspaper, a place for people to post their opinions, their arguments, their grievances.

One note criticized the Pope for being the biggest sinner of them all. Another railed against an inn where the wine was watered down. Yet another complained that a certain butcher had a heavy thumb he kept on the scale. And then I saw a note that made my stomach knot up. I knew that handwriting! It was from Mom.

If the mirrors of the world would reflect truly, they would see that hope for the stars lies in men who have bold vision and can see ahead of their time. And in one girl who is brave and true. She knows where she belongs and must go there.

What did Mom mean? She was writing in some weird code, which I guessed she had to do, posting this in public for anyone to read. I had to be the girl who was brave and true. It sounded like she was telling me to go back to the present. I reached for the note, peeling it gently from the statue. My knuckles grazed the stone.

Purple light blazed around me, and the sun wheeled overhead at dizzying speed, chased by the moon and stars. I closed my eyes, trying to still the shaking in my knees.

March 7, 1616

When I dared to look again, the world had settled around me, but I wasn't back in the present, in my right time, the way I expected. The strange statue in front of me was still covered with papers criticizing the pope, only now there were also poems defending Galileo and silly rhymes making fun of some hack painter named Baglione who was called a heap of baloney.

My stomach knotted with fear—did this mean I was supposed to save Galileo after all? It couldn't be a coincidence that there were so many notes about him. He had to be in trouble.

Only all I could think of was Bruno. He was dead, but there was still something I could do for him, if it wasn't too late.

I headed for Del Monte's. And this time, I went to the main door, the one for guests, not caring if I looked like a servant. Only I didn't! I wasn't wearing the tunic and cloak from before.

Now I was dressed in the elegant clothes Caravaggio had given me when I posed for his picture. I looked like a young nobleman! I shook my head, startled. Had I done this somehow? Figured out how to dress to my advantage? Was I learning to control reality with my thoughts after all?

A servant opened the door as soon as I knocked on it.

"I'm Marco, here to see the cardinal," I said, trying to look important with my chin in the air. Did I need a last name? Didn't people just use places for that, like Leonardo from Vinci? "Marco da San Francisco," I offered. It sounded convincing to me.

The servant led me into a spacious room glowing with late-afternoon light. A harpsichord stood in one corner with lutes leaning on the wall nearby. Above them, I recognized the first painting I'd seen by Caravaggio—*Rest on the Flight to Egypt*, the one where Giovanni was an angel playing the violin. Across from it was another picture that looked like it was by Caravaggio—this one of a fortune-teller reading the palm of a young gentleman. He was wearing a yellow tunic very similar to the one I had on! I squirmed in embarrassment. I was wearing an artist's props! What if Del Monte recognized the clothes?

I was thinking about sneaking out when the door opened and Del Monte hobbled in, much older now and leaning on a cane. How much time had passed? How could I explain that I hadn't aged when he so obviously had? I scrambled to come up with an explanation as a second man followed the cardinal into the room. I didn't recognize the newcomer, a middle-aged man with a pointy beard and mustache, making his sly face look even more like a fox.

"Marco da San Francisco?" Del Monte asked. He looked confused, like he couldn't place the name. And then his brow unfurrowed. "Marco!" he repeated, this time a declaration, not a question. "You can't be Marco. He was a youth when last I saw him. By now he'd be much older than you."

I stood up and bowed nervously. "Monsignore, Marco was my father, and I'm Marco, too. He told me about you and that I should seek you out when I came to Rome." He probably thought I wanted a job, but he had the graciousness not to say so. Instead he introduced me to the fox-faced man.

"Welcome, young Marco. This is a fellow cardinal, Scipione Borghese, the Pope's nephew."

I lowered my eyes, more anxious than ever. "An honor, Monsignore." How could I ask about Bruno, about the Inquisition, in front of a member of the Pope's family?

"Sit, relax, you're among friends here," Del Monte said. "Now, tell me why you're here."

"There are a couple of reasons, actually," I said, trying not to stare at Borghese's devilish goatee. The two men sat across from me in velvet-upholstered chairs. "First, my father wondered if you had news of Caravaggio." I wanted to hear about Giovanni, too, but how could I ask about a servant?

"Ah, then you don't know?" Borghese said.

"Know what?" It didn't sound like good news from his tone.

"He died, six years ago now. It's a sad story for one so brilliant to end his life alone, far from Rome."

"What happened?"

"He was on a boat, coming back to Rome, when the boat left him behind by mistake in Port Ercole." Borghese sounded matter-of-fact, not at all sad. "He got sick there and died of a fever."

Del Monte's face looked tight and wary. Clearly that wasn't the whole story. "His paintings survive, however," he said, changing the subject. "In fact, that's why his eminence

is here today. He came to show off Caravaggio's last painting, sent as a gift to the cardinal." Del Monte pointed to a painting I hadn't noticed before. It wasn't hanging on the wall, but leaned against a chest near the door. It showed a young man with a sad, thoughtful expression holding up the head of a bearded man, eyes bulging in the horror of death.

I studied both of the faces, a sense of dread filling me. "That's him, isn't it?" I asked, remembering the shield Caravaggio had shown me when we first met, the one with himself painted as Medusa's decapitated head. "That's Caravaggio as a young man holding the head, and him when he's older as the cut-off head."

"So it is!" Borghese exclaimed. "The artist as David *and* Goliath! He was an idealistic youth, slaying fiends, and a monster deserving death, both at the same time." The cardinal stroked his pointy beard, eyes sparkling with excitement in a beadily disturbing way. Something about this man creeped me out.

"But that's so sad!" I couldn't help blurting out.

"He was a brilliant artist but not a happy man." Del Monte sighed. "I'm sorry I couldn't give you better news of him."

"I'll leave you now to catch up with your old friend's son," Borghese said, clearly bored with the conversation now that he'd delivered his bad news. "We can discuss our business later." He heaved his bulk up from the chair. I stood up nervously, trying to be polite.

When we were alone, Del Monte cleared his throat, waiting. I sat down again, not sure how to start.

"Are you and Cardinal Borghese good friends?" I asked, wondering what business he could possibly have with the man.

"Not at all." Del Monte sounded disgusted. "The man wants to buy paintings from me, though really he came to gloat, to show off the treasure he got from poor Caravaggio, when he's the one who killed him."

"Borghese killed him?" I felt sick that I'd been polite to a murderer.

"Not directly, but he was behind it all. It's a long, complicated story, but I can give you the short version."

I nodded, numb with horror.

"Caravaggio had a temper—you must know that. After all, your father was thrown into prison with him. He picked one fight too many and killed a man by accident."

"Caravaggio was a murderer?" I felt even sicker.

"It was an accident. And the man he killed was a brutal murderer himself. Here's where Borghese enters the story. He wanted Caravaggio beholden to him so he could get pictures from him cheaply, so he convinced the Pope to condemn the painter to death."

"He couldn't paint if he was dead!"

"No, of course not, so Borghese helped smuggle Caravaggio out of Rome and sent him to Malta, the island which is run by Catholic warrior monks, telling him that he would work to reverse the Pope's judgment. In the meantime, Caravaggio could paint plenty of pictures and send them to his patron, Borghese."

I'd never heard of Malta or warrior monks and the whole story sounded ridiculously convoluted, but I believed Del Monte.

"Years later, several paintings later, Borghese sent the promised pardon to Caravaggio. Who did indeed feel grateful and painted this one last sad picture for the despicable man."

"But then why kill him?"

"Borghese didn't mean it to happen, but Caravaggio fell ill on the way back to Rome and ended up dying, probably from malaria, in a miserable town down the coast. So you see why I hold Borghese responsible. He's connived his way into the greatest art collection ever."

It was a horrible story and for a minute I wondered if that was the history I was meant to change. But I thought of Mom's note. She wrote about "men who have bold vision and can see ahead of their time." That meant Bruno. I had to remember my task, the one that only a girl who was brave and true could do.

"It's sad about Caravaggio," I said finally, "but worse about Bruno. My father admired him tremendously. He was a great man who didn't deserve to die."

Del Monte looked pained. This wasn't a subject he wanted to discuss.

"I have to ask you what happened to his books." I leaned forward urgently, lowering my voice even though Borghese had left. "You told my father years ago that if Bruno didn't recant, the Inquisition would order them destroyed. Is that what happened? Is it too late to save his work, his ideas?"

Del Monte's face sagged in sadness. He nodded slowly. "His books were put on the banned list and everyone was ordered to burn all copies."

"Did you?" I asked, praying fervently that he wasn't an obedient cardinal. "Did you actually do that? Did you save anything?"

Del Monte stared at the floor, silent, his face a mask of stillness.

"Please tell me you kept his books! You could easily hide them until the times changed, until it was safe to read them!"

There was a long silence. I held my breath until the cardinal slowly nodded.

"You saved them!" I grinned, giddy with happiness. Who knew that books could matter so much?

Del Monte looked up, his face still sad. "For what good? They'll turn to dust in my attic. Books are living things. They must be read."

"Then let them be read. Give them to somebody who will appreciate Bruno's ideas, his brilliance." And then it hit me. I knew why I was here, what I had to do. "My father sent me for just this reason. I can be the courier, giving them to your friend, to Galileo. He'll take Bruno's theories and expand on them."

A slow smile bloomed on Del Monte's face. "Funny you should say that. Galileo is here now, you know, in Rome."

"Really? Why?" I hoped he wasn't in prison, waiting to be burned at the stake, like Bruno.

"He thinks he can convince the Pope that Copernicus' theory isn't heresy, that the earth orbits the sun instead of the other way around."

My stomach twisted. So Galileo did need my help or he'd be burned at the stake like Bruno.

"Will the Pope listen?"

"He'll listen, but he won't agree." I must have looked as sick as I felt, because Del Monte rushed to reassure me. "Don't worry. I know Galileo well. He has no wish to contradict the Church. He'll insist this is all a simple misunderstanding."

"So then he won't be put in prison?" I asked.

"I think not," Del Monte said. "And I think you're right. I should profit from his presence here to give him an invaluable gift. Bruno's books belong with Galileo. He'll take good care of them so that future generations will be able to read Bruno's ideas."

"We could do even more," I suggested, suddenly remembering our earlier conversation. "We could smuggle some of them to Switzerland. You said, I mean, my father said, there are presses there that print banned books. That way everyone could read Bruno. Long after the Inquisition is over, Bruno's ideas will live."

Del Monte gave me a long, slow look. "Your father has

exceptional interests. I'm sorry I didn't get to know him better the short time he was here."

I tried to calm the blush rising up my cheeks. "My father was very impressed by you, by how you tried to help Bruno. And he was forever changed by his reading of Bruno's manuscript."

Del Monte nodded. "He was a brilliant man. And your idea is sound. There's a big business in banned books, all coming from Switzerland, but how do we get the books there? Who would risk carrying them there?"

"I would!" I sat up proudly. Here, finally, was a clear task, something I could do. Once I figured out how to hitch a ride to Switzerland. Or found another way to get the books to a good printer.

Del Monte's eyes glowed. He looked ten years younger than when he'd come into the room, like a great burden had been lifted.

"Some things have to wait for the future to be truly appreciated. Like my friend Caravaggio." He gestured toward the painting of David and Goliath. "And the brilliant Giordano Bruno. Wait here while I get you my copies of Bruno's works."

"Thank you, Monsignore," I murmured. "I'll be on my way as soon as I have them." Alone in the room, I stared again at Caravaggio's paintings. Looking at the first one I'd seen, the holy family, I was struck once more by how much care the artist had taken with every object in the scene. The blades of grass, the leaves, the pebbles all held the same weight, the same attention as the Virgin Mary and the Christ Child. It was like Bruno's ideas made visual! Everything made of the same building blocks, only taking different forms, everything full of the same sense of the divine.

"Caravaggio, you sneaky devil," I whispered under my breath. "You were as much of a heretic as Bruno. Perhaps your death wasn't from sickness after all." I smiled, thinking of his picture belonging to Cardinal Borghese now. The Pope's own nephew was housing rebellious works of art. He was just too dense to realize it.

Del Monte returned with a satchel full of books, reminding me of the task ahead. "Be careful," he said. "I've saved a couple to pass on to Galileo, but these are true treasures, ones that must get safely to Switzerland, either Geneva or Basel."

"I know their value." I took the leather bag. "And soon so will the whole world."

I left the palazzo in a daze. I'd done something! I was making a difference! I was saving the most important part of Bruno!

I looked up, suddenly aware that I was by the church that Malcolm, Dad, and I had gone into, the one with the Caravaggio paintings.

An old beggar woman sat by the doorway, her cupped hand held out while she whined in a nasal monotone, *"Per pieta, signori, per pieta.* Have pity, have pity, have pity!"

I didn't want to get close to her, but I wanted to go in, to see those powerful paintings again. I started to edge by her, ignoring her plea when she shot out her bony hand and grabbed my ankle.

"Let me go!" I kicked angrily. "Let go!"

"No! I told you not to interfere, but you don't listen!" It was the Watcher! With the scarf fallen off her head, she wasn't old or ugly anymore, but beautiful and young. And strong. I tried to wrench myself free, to tear away her hand, but I couldn't loosen her grip.

"I didn't do anything!" I kicked at her, flailing to try to get her to release me.

"Unhand the young man!" a deep voice called out. The Watcher quickly let go, pulling her scarf back over her head, transforming herself in seconds into a harmless old woman.

I bolted down the church steps, looking for the person the voice belonged to, but I didn't see anyone. The edge of a cape flapped around the corner of a building and I dashed after it, expecting to find Morton, or maybe even Mom. Who else would save me? But if it was either of them, I lost their trail in front of the Pantheon. I stopped to catch my breath, struck as always by the perfect balance and calm of the ancient domed temple.

A man emerged from the darkness of the interior. His golden curls caught the light, and as he turned to face me, I stared, struck by his resemblance to Giovanni. He was older, thicker, and a scar cleft his chin, but it could be him.

Heart thumping, I walked over to the man. I had to know for sure if it was him.

"Excuse me, sir, but are you Giovanni, once the servant of Caravaggio?" I asked.

"Who wants to know?" The man tilted back his chin, and in that gesture, I had my answer.

"I'm Marco, the son of the Marco that you knew for a short while many years ago, the scribe who worked for Del Monte."

"Marco? Ah, Marco! He survived the galleys? He had a son?" Giovanni's face split into a wide smile. "Welcome to Rome, Marco the younger. I'm happy to meet you."

"As am I!" I grinned stupidly, then remembered what the cardinal had just told me. "I come from Del Monte's, where I heard what happened to Caravaggio. I'm so sorry!"

Giovanni shrugged. "These past years haven't been easy since I lost that position. I'm tired of sleeping on tavern floors or in stables. In fact I was thinking of going home, back to my village. Unless you need a servant. You look like a man who can afford one."

Me? With a servant? I laughed, but when I saw the look of hurt flash across Giovanni's face, I felt terrible. "I'm not

laughing because you're a bad servant, Giovanni. My father…"
Again I had to explain everything through a third person. "My
father told me how much you helped him when he first came
to Rome, how you were his only real friend."

Giovanni brightened. "He mentioned me to you?"

"Of course! You were very important to him and that makes
you important to me." The weight of the satchel on my shoulder gave me an idea. "I can't use you as a servant, but I can
propose another job for you."

"Anything!" Giovanni said eagerly. "So long as the work
is steady."

"Would you be interested in delivering these books to
a printer in Switzerland? Tell them they can have them in
exchange for taking you on as an apprentice. That way you'll
have a new position and the books will be taken care of."

"A printer? Which printer?"

"It doesn't matter which. Del Monte tells me that Geneva
and Basel are home to many small presses and that any one
of them would be happy to make copies of these books. Ask
around. Find one that will take you
on." I handed over my valuable
cargo. "But promise me you'll be
careful. These books are like
your master's paintings, full
of the same kind of ideas."

Giovanni scratched his head. "I don't see how a book can be like a picture, but I'm willing to make the journey." He took the satchel from me, and I felt a lightness flood my body. This was the right thing to do.

"Good-bye, then, and Godspeed." I clasped Giovanni's hand in my own and pulled him close for a last hug. I would miss him, but at least this time I could say a proper good-bye.

Alone again, I wove through the streets, looking for a touchstone. I'd done what I could and it was time to go home. I found my way back to the statue with the notes posted around it. For once I felt confident, like I'd done what I needed to do, as I reached out and touched the cold stone. And the world spilled away from me in a swirl of stardust, of black and purple pulsing clouds.

I took a deep breath. I was in my regular clothes and the statue was still there, only now the notes were written in Sharpie or ballpoint pen. Now they criticized the Italian government for being corrupt, for turning its back on the people. There were still notes mocking the Pope. I couldn't help smiling. Some things don't change, I thought.

I walked back to Campo de' Fiori, intensely grateful that this was my time, this was where I belonged. The tourists in their shorts and bright T-shirts looked friendly and beautiful, even the hordes following tour guides.

Back in the piazza, the market stalls

looked cheerful, and the statue of Bruno seemed proud and serene, not tortured at all. I smiled at the hooded face. "You're still here," I whispered to him. "Your ideas are still alive. That's something."

"Where did you go?" Malcolm asked. "I turned around and you'd vanished."

I rolled my eyes. "You should know what that means by now."

"What did you see?" he asked, his eyebrows pitched up in worry.

"Him." I turned my chin up toward Bruno. "Being burned at the stake. I couldn't stop it! It was horrible!"

"That's awful!" Malcolm's face crumpled in horror. He stared at the statue, as if he was imagining it in flames.

"He had so many brilliant theories. I want to see if I can find his books, if they escaped the Inquisition." The way they should have, I thought.

"It makes you wonder, doesn't it," said Malcolm. "How many other great thinkers or inventors were time travelers? Maybe that's where the best ideas came from. Maybe Edison, Einstein, and Tesla were all time travelers!"

"Maybe some great writers, too," I agreed. "Like Jules Verne, Isaac Asimov, H. G. Wells. Maybe people who wrote about time travel were describing the truth instead of making things up."

"That's a scary thought!"

"Where's Dad?" I scanned the market. There he was, buying

olives by the ladle-full. "Come on," I said to Malcolm. "I have a note from Mom." It was still in my fingers from when I'd taken it off the statue in 1600. I showed it to Malcolm.

"Sounds like she wanted you back here."

"That's what I thought. But first I saw Del Monte again."

I told Dad and Malcolm about that last visit. About Caravaggio's painting. About Cardinal Borghese. And, most important, about Del Monte saving Bruno's books, passing them on to Galileo and farther, on to Switzerland where many copies could be made with the printing presses there.

Dad put his arm around me. "I'm proud of you, Mira. You helped move science and liberal thinking forward. You kept important ideas alive."

I snuggled into his chest. I was actually proud of myself, too.

"Yeah," Malcolm agreed. "The Inquisition won in the short term, but in the long term religious narrowness and extremism were defeated. Didn't the Age of Enlightenment come right after the Renaissance?"

"Look around you," Dad said. "We're in the heart of the papacy, and where's that religious extremism now? Rome is a beautiful city, rich with churches and all kinds of freedoms. People can say what they think, believe what they want."

We walked slowly, dreamily as the sun lowered in the sky. Our shadows stretched in front of us, as we ambled through the Forum, through the past, all the way to the Colosseum.

"Remember when it was the Christians being tortured?" Dad said as he framed the stadium with his camera. "Then they were the ones doing the torture in the Inquisition. It's all part of a progression, and tolerance is winning. You helped it win."

I wished I could be as sure as him. I knew I'd helped Bruno, even Galileo, but seeing the Inquisition firsthand, feeling its power, made it hard to forget what that kind of tyranny could do.

I looked at the sun, dipping ever lower. I couldn't help thinking that it did look like it moved across the sky. No wonder people thought for so long that that meant the earth stood still. We can only see as far as our experience allows us. I wondered what ideas I had that were totally wrong, the same way people once believed that the earth was flat. What things did I take for gospel that were really pure speculation, opinion, not fact?

We walked back to the hotel, taking a detour to pass St. Peter's on our way. It was no longer a symbol of worldly power. It was simply a beautiful building. There was still a pope, but he didn't have much power to hurt anyone anymore.

"You know," Malcolm said, staring at St. Peter's, "Galileo

wasn't executed. He recanted, the way Bruno wouldn't. And Pope John Paul II admitted that the Church was wrong to try Galileo. He actually offered a formal apology. Five hundred years later!"

I smiled. It was almost as if he'd read my mind. "What about Bruno?"

"Nope," Malcolm shook his head. "No apology for him. He's still considered a terrible heretic by the Church. A hero to the people who put up the statue, but not to the Pope."

"And," added Dad, "a brilliant mind. You have to wonder if there would have been a Galileo without a Bruno." Dad pulled me close in a one-armed hug as we faced the great dome. "I'm proud that you got to meet him, that you want to read his books. They survived, you know. You can even read them online."

I nodded, relieved, happy that the most important part of Bruno was still here, alive and well in my time.

"And what about Mom?" I asked. "She told me to come home but didn't say anything about herself. I didn't even get a chance to warn her about the Watcher."

"She'll let us know where we need to go next," Dad said. "And we'll be there, right?"

I snuggled under the crook of his arm, feeling safe and warm. "I hope it's someplace far from any Inquisition and popes and churches." I had a hunch we'd be getting another postcard soon. Where would we be going next? What would I have to do?

"Hmmm…Indonesia? Morocco? Peru?" Malcolm suggested. "Asia! There's no pope there."

"Knowing your mother, it will be a place with a wonder," Dad said.

"There's always the Great Wall of China—that's a good wonder," said Malcolm.

"Not for me!" I objected. I didn't want to go back in time to the Mongol hordes killing their way through Asia. Bruno's death was enough. "Let's pick a peaceful place, someplace where nothing bad has ever happened."

"It's peaceful here, now," Dad said. We crossed the Bridge of Angels as the moon rose over St. Peter's. You'd never know that decapitated heads of criminals once lined the bridge, that executions took place right in front of the Castel Sant'Angelo. The biggest hazard now was pigeon droppings. I hoped wherever Mom was, she was safe. And that someday soon, we'd all be together as a family again. No more wonders, no more time travel, just a regular family doing ordinary things. That was marvelous enough for me.

Author's Note

While Mira and her adventures are invented, the places she visits are all real. The meridian in Santa Maria degli Angeli was commissioned by Pope Clement XI in the early eighteenth century. Francesco Bianchini, an astronomer, mathematician, archeologist, historian, and philosopher (a true jack-of-all-trades) created the device to measure the accuracy of the recently reformed Gregorian calendar, to predict when Easter would fall, and to rival the meridian line in Bologna's cathedral.

The church of Santa Maria degli Angeli was chosen because it was once part of the ancient Roman baths of the emperor Diocletian and would symbolize how the Christian era, represented by the Christian calendar, triumphed over pagan times. Along with the meridian, Bianchini included a sun-dial measuring the summer and winter solstices, the equinox, and the passage of two major stars, Arcturus and Sirius. The meridian was restored in 2002 and still functions today.

Many of the people Mira encounters also really existed. Cardinal Francesco Maria Bourbon Del Monte was an important supporter of art and science, a patron of both Galileo and Caravaggio. Del Monte was actually given a telescope by Galileo, but later than 1595 when Mira first meets him. The refracting telescope was invented by Hans Lippershy in 1608 (or at least patented by him then), and Galileo developed his own to use for astronomical observations in 1609. I've telescoped the dates for dramatic reasons.

Del Monte's home, Palazzo Madama on via del Rinascimento in Rome, is now the Italian Senate building. While the cardinal intended to be buried in nearby San Luigi dei Francesi, his funeral was there while his body was interred in Sant'Urbano di Roma.

Giordano Bruno was a brilliant writer and philosopher, burned at the stake for heresy as described here. He was fascinated with many areas of study, from optics to mathematics to physics. He probably learned about atoms from Lucretius in his book, *On the Nature of Things*. While popularized by the Roman Lucretius, the theory of atoms originated in ancient Greece with Democritus and his mentor, Leucippus.

The idea that the same small particles in different combinations make up all matter jibed with Bruno's sense that everything was part of the divine, that there was no material separation between man, beast, and angel. This concept was only one of the many notions the Inquisition considered heretical. A statue in Bruno's honor still stands in the middle of the Campo de' Fiori in Rome.

The passage quoted here from Bruno's book was translated by Lisa Kaborycha and appears in her book, *A Short History of Renaissance Italy*. I am indebted to her for her advice and the rich resources she provides on her website.

While Bruno refused to recant and died for his beliefs, Galileo gave in to the Inquisition and admitted that his ideas were only theories, not science. He was held under house arrest for the rest of his days, even requiring special permission to go to Easter services. Pope John Paul II issued a formal apology in 2000, more than 350 years after the original trial, for the condemnation and punishment that Galileo suffered. No such apology has been given to Bruno.

The Jewish community in Rome is the oldest in Europe, neither Sephardic nor Ashkenzic, but unique to itself. While eastern European Jews spoke Yiddish and Spanish Jews spoke Landino, the Roman Jews still speak their own language, "judaico romanesco."

For nearly two thousand years, the Arch of Titus, commemorating the Roman victory over Judea under the emperor Vespasian, has been a symbol of Jewish loss. For centuries, Roman Jews would not pass underneath it, reading the imagery of the stolen menorah and the Jewish captives as a parable for their own exile from Jerusalem. In the nineteenth century, this symbol of shame was transformed into one of pride, a marker of Jewish redemption in exile.

The Fourth Lateran Council in 1215 decreed that Jews throughout Europe had to wear distinctive clothing so their identity would be obvious. The "sign of the Jew" was originally a yellow cloth circle (the origin for the later Nazi star), but that was considered too easily hidden, so in the sixteenth century, a yellow hat was implemented instead. The Jewish badge was imposed in England, France, Germany, Hungary, and Spain right after the council, but Italy, despite being home to the Vatican, generally ignored the decree until the fifteenth century.

In 1555, the Roman ghetto was established, modeled after the earlier ghetto in Venice. The Jewish community was forced to live in a walled area so close to the banks of the Tiber that thousands of houses were flooded when the Tiber overflowed its banks. The gates were opened in the morning, and those with passes were allowed out, only to be locked back in at night when the gates were closed. Even after Italy was united as a county and the Papacy relegated to Vatican City in 1870, Jews were still required to live in the ghetto until 1881, and the walls were finally destroyed only in 1888. The Roman ghetto was the last remaining one in Europe until the Nazis reintroduced them in the 1930s.

The Roman Inquisition spared the Jews for the most part, despite the baptistery used for forced conversion that still stands in the ghetto. Compared to the Spanish Inquisition, the Roman version was mild, though Giordano Bruno might disagree.

The Church's reaction to American nuns, the Leadership Council of Women Religious, eerily echoes its attitude toward Bruno. The nuns ask if you can be a good Catholic and have a questioning mind, if you can raise questions on issues of faith and justice and search for truth. The answer from the all-male cardinals is a resounding no.

All the artists mentioned are real, as are their works, from Michelangelo's design of the Capitoline piazza to Caravaggio's last painting of David and Goliath. The incident with the artichokes actually happened, and Del Monte's description of Caravaggio's death follows the general lines of his last years.

Map of Rome

1. Bridge of Angels
2. Castel Sant'Angelo
3. Tor di Nona Prison
4. Caravaggio's rented house
5. Column of Marcus Aurelius
6. Trevi fountain
7. Pantheon
8. Palazzo Madama
9. Forum
10. Colosseum
11. Ghetto
12. Statue of Giordano Bruno in Campo de Fiori
13. Pasquino

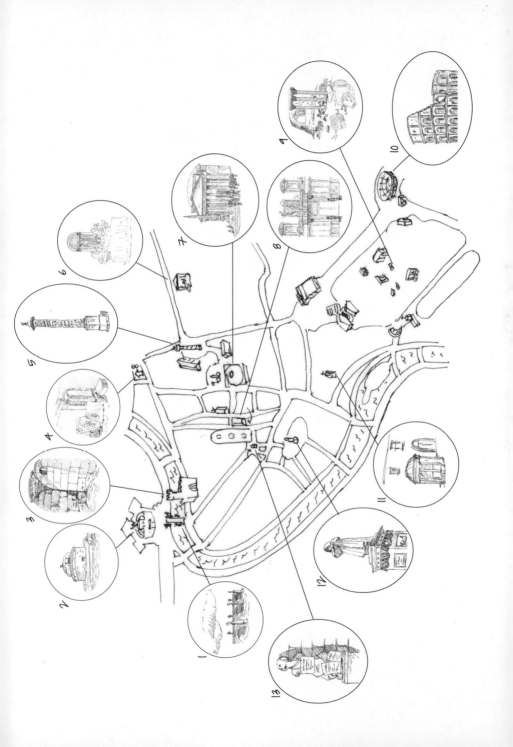

Bibliography

Bruno, Giordano. *The Expulsion of the Triumphant Beast.* Lincoln, NE: Bison Books, 2004.

da Caravaggio, Michelangelo Merisi. *Caravaggio a Roma, Una Vita dal Vero.* Rome: Archivio di Stato di Roma, 2011.

Galilei, Galileo. *The Essential Galileo.* Edited by Maurice A. Finocchiaro. Cambridge, MA: Hackett Publishing Co., 2008.

Gatti, Hilary. *Giordano Bruno and Renaissance Science.* Ithaca, NY: Cornell University Press, 2002.

Greenblatt, Stephen. *The Swerve: How the World Became Modern.* New York: W.W. Norton, 2012.

Heilbron, J. L. *Galileo.* New York: Oxford University Press, 2010.

Hibbard, Howard, and Shirley G. Hibbard. *Caravaggio.* Boulder, CO: Westview Press, 1985.

Kaborycha, Lisa. *A Short History of Renaissance Italy.* New York: Prentice Hall, 2011.

Lucretius. *The Nature of Things*. Translated by Alicia Stalling. New York: Penguin Classics, 2007.

Mancini, Giorgio, Giovanni Baglione, and Giovanni Pietro Bellori. *The Lives of Caravaggio*. London: Pallas Athene, 2005.

Partner, Peter. *Renaissance Rome 1500-1559: A Portrait of a Society*. Berkeley: University of California Press, 1980.

Rowland, Ingrid. *Giordano Bruno: Philosopher/Heretic*. Chicago: University of Chicago Press, 2009.

Shea, William R., and Mariano Artigas. *Galileo in Rome: The Rise and Fall of a Troublesome Genius*. New York: Oxford University Press, 2004.

Spike, John T. *Caravaggio*. New York: Abbeville Press, 2010.

Vodret, Rossella, and Francesco Buranelli, eds. *Caravaggio*. Milan: Skira, 2010.

White, Michael. *The Pope and the Heretic: The True Story of Giordano Bruno, the Man Who Dared to Defy the Roman Inquisition*. New York: Little, Brown & Co., 2002.

About the Author

Marissa Moss has published more than 50 children's books, and her illustrated Amelia's Notebook series has sold more than two million copies. Although she hopes to visit all the wonders of the world, right now she lives in the San Francisco Bay area, where she can appreciate the Golden Gate Bridge from her window. Visit www.marissamoss.com for more.